William J. Reid, D.D.

Quarter centennial anniversary of the installation

William J. Reid, D.D.

Quarter centennial anniversary of the installation

ISBN/EAN: 9783741195136

Manufactured in Europe, USA, Canada, Australia, Japa

Cover: Foto ©Andreas Hilbeck / pixelio.de

Manufactured and distributed by brebook publishing software
(www.brebook.com)

William J. Reid, D.D.

Quarter centennial anniversary of the installation

Quarter Centennial Anniversary

OF THE

Installation

OF

Rev. William J. Reid, D.D.,

AS PASTOR OF THE

First United Presbyterian Church,

Pittsburgh, Pa.,

Thursday, April 7th, 1887.

———

PITTSBURGH, PA.:
PRESS OF STEVENSON & FOSTER, 529 WOOD STREET.
MDCCCLXXXVII.

THE FIRST UNITED PRESBYTERIAN CHURCH, OF PITTSBURGH, PA.

OFFICERS OF THE CONGREGATION.

THE PASTOR.

William J. Reid, D. D.

THE SESSION.

William J. Reid, Moderator,	Samuel George,
S. L. McHenry, Clerk,	W. A. Edeburn,
J. G. Templeton, Treasurer,	Thomas A. Elliott,

William C. Shaw.

THE TRUSTEES.

A. M. Brown, President,	Thomas R. Herd,
Robert J. McKnight, Secretary,	Frank G. Bryce,
James Loughridge, Treasurer,	E. B. Mahood,

Samuel McMahon.

THE SABBATH SCHOOL.

J. G. Templeton, Superintendent,	Jas. Loughridge, 2d Ass't.Sup't.,
W. A. Edeburn, 1st Ass't. Sup't.,	G. Lambert Rodgers, Treasurer.

TEACHERS IN THE ADVANCED DEPARTMENT,

William J. Reid,	Miss Sarah Irvine,
Miss Annie M. Adams,	Robert W. Stewart.

TEACHERS IN THE INTERMEDIATE DEPARTMENT.

S. L. McHenry,	Mrs. Anna M. Sturtevant,
Miss Sarah J. McIlwain,	Miss J. L. Brownlee,
Robert McBride,	Mrs. Maggie J. Hill,
Miss Lizzie McMillan,	Miss Maggie Duncan,

Miss Mary McQuigg.

TEACHERS IN THE PRIMARY DEPARTMENT.

Mrs. Mary B. Reid, Superintendent,	Miss Maggie Martin,
Mrs. Mary S. Stevenson,	Miss Maria S. Moffat,
Mrs. Nancy Large,	Miss Jennie E. Thompson,
Mrs. Mary Bryce,	Miss Della D. McHenry,
Miss Hattie Creighton,	Miss Hattie J. Creque.

Quarter Centennial Anniversary.

The First United Presbyterian Church is one of the oldest of the churches of Pittsburgh. It was organized, Nov. 17, 1801, by the election of Ruling Elders, under the name of "The Associate Congregation of Pittsburgh." During its history, it has had six pastors: Rev. Ebenezer Henderson, installed in the summer of 1802, released April 13, 1804, died Sept. 17, 1804; Rev. Robert Bruce, D. D., ordained and installed, Dec. 14, 1808, died June 14, 1846; Rev. Abraham Anderson, ordained and installed Sept., 1847, died July 27, 1849; Rev. Hans W. Lee, ordained and installed in the summer of 1850, released in the spring of 1855, died Oct. 12, 1855; Rev. Samuel B. Reed, D. D., ordained and installed April 29, 1857, released July 11, 1859, died April 10, 1884. On Sept. 12, 1861, a call was made out for William J. Reid, a licentiate under the care of the Presbytery of Argyle. He accepted this call, Dec. 31, 1861, and was ordained and installed pastor of the congregation, April 7, 1862, Rev. James Prestley, D. D., presiding, Rev. W. H. Andrews, D. D., preaching the sermon, Rev. Robert Gracey, D. D., addressing the pastor, and Rev. A. Y. Houston, addressing the congregation.

As the twenty-fifth anniversary of this installation approached, the congregation determined to celebrate it with appropriate exercises. Committees were appointed and arrangements were made. On April 7, 1887, in the Church, corner of Seventh Avenue and Cherry Alley, the "Silver Wedding" of the First United Presbyterian

Church and its pastor was celebrated. The audience room was tastefully decorated with tropical plants, wreaths and flowers. Among other decorations, there was a floral shield on each side of the pulpit ; one bearing the dates, " 1862–1887 ;" the other the words, "Remembering without ceasing your work of faith and labor of love." A. M. BROWN, ESQ., presided. Two sessions were held, one in the afternoon and the other in the evening. A large congregation was present and deep interest was taken in the exercises.

AFTERNOON SESSION.

After an Anthem by the Choir and the reading of a Scripture Lesson by Rev. J. D. TURNER, pastor of the Fourth United Presbyterian Church, the congregation joined in singing Psalm 100, L. M. Prayer was then offered by Rev. H. C. MARSHALL, of the Oakland Chapel, when the Chairman made the Introductory Address.

INTRODUCTORY ADDRESS,

BY A. M. BROWN, ESQ., CHAIRMAN.

We are assembled to commemorate the twenty-fifth Anniversary of Dr. Wm. J. Reid's pastorate of The First United Presbyterian Church of Pittsburgh. Speaking for the congregation, as I am privileged and pleased to do, I extend to each of our visiting friends and guests a cordial welcome. Our hearts would shake hands with all of you. We are jubilant to-day ! Our hearts are overflowing with gratitude to God for the growth and prosperity we have attained within the quarter of a century just closed ; for the peace, brotherly love and happiness we have enjoyed as a congregation, and for all that our honored and loved pastor has been, and is, as our teacher, leader and friend !

My admiration for Dr. Reid—and I but voice the sentiment of all hearts within our congregation and an innumerable multitude without— my admiration for Dr. Reid is so great that, like a child speaking of a loving father, I can scarcely restrain my words or control "the lava-tide of burning thoughts" that presses upon me. No pastor has ever possessed in larger, fuller and more rounded measure, the confidence and love of his congregation; and I can truly say that, whilst his teaching has been of the wisest and ablest, his conduct and personal example within and without the church have been so gentle, upright, and pure, and his life so self-sacrificing and devoted to the interests and welfare of his people and to the service of the Master, that all have learned to know him but to love him, and to name him but to praise,

"The changeless, sure,
And genial friend, to many hearts how dear."

Expressing the earnest sentiment of our hearts, measured and approved by intelligent and deliberate judgment, we cannot fail to say that he is not merely great in natural force and mental acquirements, but truly and eminently great in that applied strength which carries up most hearts by the attraction of his own—a divinely gifted man. Kindly and highly as we can and do speak of the historical names of the earlier pastors of this church, whose life-work is their imperishable memorial, we are altogether convinced that none of his illustrious predecessors has been, or could have been, more able, sincere, and faithful, and certainly no administration of the pastorate has ever been more fruitful or successful than the present.

It may be truly and fitly said of Dr. Reid, as it is recorded in sacred history of the good Judean King, Hezekiah, that "in every work that he began, he did it with all his heart, and prospered." The Egyptians of old had a custom of trying their public men *after death*, and recording their merits and demerits by a sentence pronounced after full hearing of all except the party tried. Our plan is more practical and better. We grant a fair public trial in life, face to face with the living witnesses and before competent tribunals, whether a local or limited forum or the bar of the world. This is certainly better and safer than traditional testimony and posthumous eulogy, which are often, if not always, doubtful and suspicious. Dr. Reid, in his high office, has been on trial in this church, and before the world, for a quarter of a century, and the unanimous verdict of a grateful people crowns him with immortal honor. "Remembering, without ceasing, his work of faith and labor of love," we are here to-day to enter judgment on that verdict without denial or delay! But our friend and pastor has laid only the foundation of his great monument; he will, I trust, live many years more to carry the beautiful and perfect structure to its utmost height.   Of course I speak not of material monuments.   The vast pyramids of Egypt are material wonders, but they have no significance and are valueless to the human race.   Monuments may be builded to express the affection and pride of friends, or to display their wealth, but they are only valuable when they teach impressive lessons of useful and successful lives.   Our honored pastor will need no such material memorial.   He will live in the hearts of the people who worship here, in the present and in the future, and his praise will be in all the churches. He will be assigned his high place in that not innumerable caravan of those whose true memorial is a world made better by their lives.

But, whilst we all realize the solemn truth that

> *   *   *   " Time is fleeting,
> And our hearts, though stout and brave,
> Still, like muffled drums, are beating
>   Funeral marches to the grave,"

we are not here to-day to mar the bright sunlight of the living present, by sad musings or gloomy thoughts.   Our pastor is yet in the prime of vigorous life.   Let not his prematurely silvered head deceive you.   That good gray head is neither old in years nor weakened in intellectual power; never before was he so great and able as now, and we—some of us, not all of us—may reasonably hope to be present in this temple, with a great congregation, to celebrate, fitly and joyously, the semi-centennial of his pastorate—the golden wedding of pastor and people!   In the meantime, if wrinkles must be written on our brows, let them not be written upon our hearts!   Then let us, both pastor and people, with united heart and hand, continue to

> " Act—act in the living present!
> Heart within, and God o'erhead ! "

And, in the memorable language of Dr. Reid himself, " Let us be inspired by the successes of the past to win even greater successes in the future.   May our congregation be a greater power for good than it ever has been !   May its liberality and its devotion, its faith and its holiness and its love ever go on towards perfection !   May thousands and tens of thousands rise up in coming years to bless it as their spiritual birthplace and home ;" and in the future, as in the past, may our ways be ways of pleasantness and all our paths be peace.

Now, having feebly expressed the sentiment of the congregation as to our pastor, I come to a more difficult subject.   With so great a leader, what is the character of the rank and file ?   In avoiding Scylla,

I may encounter Charybdis. If, as a truthful historian, I offend with
faint praise, charitably ascribe it to my Irish modesty. If, on the other
hand, I unduly magnify their virtues, ignoring their faults, credit it to
my Scotch audacity; for, like most of the congregation, I inherited
enough of that generous blood to give me a good start in this wicked
world! Speaking frankly, therefore, of the *men* of the congregation,
I am compelled to say that we are "no better than we should be"—
and that is a negative pregnant, a kind of Scotch verdict, that relieves
us from condemnation, without justification! We have not profited as
we might and should have done from the instruction and example of
our pastor. Still, with all our imperfections on our head, we have
greatly improved. Among other things, we have learned to know that
the government does not coin cents and nickles for the sole purpose of
enabling Christians to contribute to charitable uses! That a dollar has
more evangelizing power than a dime! Therefore we are not "Penny
Christians", although I think that the Treasurer and other fiscal agents
of the congregation are sometimes regarded as publicans and sinners,
with whom frequent contact is not desirable. In bygone days, we gathered the contributions in bags—not because they were large, but to
avoid ostentatious giving; yet I regret to say that often the bags did not
contain enough to have tempted even Judas, who, sacred history informs
us, carried the bag and was a low priced thief! We now gather the collections in baskets, although they are neither as large nor as well filled
as our market baskets, yet I hope we will soon reach a standard of liberality that will enable us to fill the baskets with good round measure
and running over, whenever we may be called upon to unload our
pockets. At first some of us were halt, if not blind, in doing our duty.
Our feeble steps are giving place to manly strides, and now you could
hardly find a weak-kneed brother in the congregation—unless, perhaps,
you carried around a subscription book for an investment that did not
promise ten per cent. dividends, free of government taxes! I would
like to say more good things of my brethren and myself, but my modesty overcomes me, and I cannot do justice to the subject.

Of the women of the congregation, however, I cannot speak too
highly. We have realized the poetic truth that women are indeed
"Heaven's last, best gift to man." With amazing brightness, purity
and truth, they lead us forward and upward! Illustrating the Christian
graces in an eminent degree, they are always in the front rank and ever
foremost as faithful, diligent and earnest workers. They heap coals of
fire on our heads, and thus the base metal in us will, I hope, soon be
removed, and only sterling qualities remain! I blush for our manly

weaknesses.   Stimulated by the noble example of the women of the
Church, we are improving and advancing.   They are far ahead, but by
and by, I hope, we will be able to catch up !

THE CHAIRMAN—The next address will be by Dr. J. C.
BOYD, pastor of the St. Clair congregation, who needs no
introduction to this, or any other Christian congregation
in our county.

LONG PASTORATES,

BY REV. J. C. BOYD, D. D.

The pastorate we commemorate to-day suggests my theme as one suit-
able for this occasion.   A pastorate of twenty-five years is a long one,
long as pastorates average these days, and long when considered with
reference to the progress of the Church and country during that period.
True, when memory runs back to that day when Monongahela Presbytery
laid ordaining hands on the head of our brother, it seems but a short
time ; so rapidly have the years rolled away ; so quickly have gray hairs
come upon us.

This pastorate which has been so long, so prosperous and so peaceful,
began in dark and stormy times.   On the seventh day of April,
eighteen hundred and sixty-two, this people could say once more, " We
have a pastor," but they hardly knew whether or not they could say,
" We have a country !"   " We have a government !"

For a year civil war had been raging.   But little progress had been
made toward putting down the rebellion.   Our eastern armies had made
no advance, and remained inactive in the face of an inferior force of
the enemy.   The light was beginning to break in the southwest, under
the lead of that mighty warrior—General Grant—whose name and fame
are the proud heritage of the nation ; Forts Henry and Donelson, with
many thousands of the enemy, had been captured ; the great battle of
Shiloh had been fought and the enemy driven back.

During the first three years of this pastorate the patriotic souls of our countrymen were sorely tried.   War, bloody, terrible, exhausting war continued to prevail.   These, now busy, streets were then very often filled with soldiers.   At times the whole loyal country was wrought up to the highest pitch of excitement.   At other times a pall, black as "midnight piled on midnight," hung over the nation.   There were days, and weeks, and months then when it was an agony to live.   Patriotic hearts were wrung with unceasing anguish.   Loyal men could say, as Paul did, "We die daily."   The condition and hopes of the nation were well expressed by her truest poet :

> "We wait beneath the furnace blast
>   The pangs of transformation ;
> Not painlessly doth God recast
>   And mould anew the nation.
>   Hot burns the fire
>   Where wrongs expire ;
>   Nor spares the hand
>   That from the land
>   Uproots the ancient evil.

*   *   *   *   *   *   *

> "Then let the selfish lip be dumb,
>   And hushed the breath of sighing ;
> Before the joy of peace must come
>   The pains of purifying.
>   God give us grace
>   Each in his place
>   To bear his lot,
>   And, murmuring not,
>   Endure and wait and labor."

Four pastorates of the length of this one fill up a century and take us back to the days of our nation's infancy.   Sixteen pastorates, each of the length of this one, reach back to the time, and beyond it, when Columbus discovered America.   Seventy-five pastorates of twenty-five years each fill up all those years of the Christian era since Jesus, twelve years of age, disputed in the temple with the doctors and lawyers!

This occasion itself—this interested Assembly, this happy congregation, these quarter-centennial exercises, all proclaim the long pastorate as deserving of recognition and honor.   If this relation of pastor and people had existed only two or three years instead of twenty-five, its celebration had never been thought of.   The Church and the world even testify their respect for pastorates of long continuance.

If that brilliant but erratic divine—Henry Ward Beecher—who lately passed away, had labored a few years in one city, and a few in

another, and another, and so on, closing his work with a pastorate four
or five years long in Plymouth Church, Brooklyn, would he have gained
the hold he evidently did gain upon the hearts of that community?
Would he have had the influence in that city he did have?

And who does not believe it is better for the name, the influence and
the fame of Dr. Storrs, of the same city, that for forty years he has stood
as an honored ambassador of Jesus Christ, preaching all those years
from the same pulpit, than if he had spent his ministerial life in a half
dozen pastorates?

And if there is one man in our whole church whom we all would
crown as *primus inter pares*, he is our honored Secretary of the Board
of Foreign Missions, who for nearly forty-seven years has held the same
pastorate in the city of Philadelphia.

The eminent fathers and leaders of our Church made but few changes
in their fields of labor. Drs. John Anderson, the elder Mason, Ramsey, Riddell, Kerr, Scroggs, Pressly, McElwee, Cooper, Grier, and your
own Bruce, all men of precious memory, were associated with long pastorates. It may be that some of the fathers looked upon the dissolution of the pastoral relation with an unnecessary degree of horror.
Perhaps they were wrong in regarding it almost as indissoluble as the
relation of husband and wife. However that may be, we all know that
the causes of short pastorates are so frequently unworthy of the pastor
or the people, that even presumptive evidence of their absence, such as
the long pastorate affords, is favorable to pastor, or people, or both.

It is freely conceded that sometimes there are good and sufficient
reasons for dissolving the pastoral relation, even but a short time after it
has been formed. But in too many cases dissolution is granted for
reasons which ought not to have an existence.

One of the most frequently named causes of short pastorates is insuf-
ficient support. True, relations are sometimes dissolved for this reason
when neither pastor nor people should be blamed. The congregation
was small and their means not great. They, in the hope of obtaining
help from the Home Mission Board, extended a call to a promising
young probationer, and he anticipating a growth that was not realized
entered the field with commendable enthusiasm. But the expectations
of both pastor and people were disappointed, and separation followed
as a natural result. The unpleasant truth however must not be denied
or disguised, that very often the relation is dissolved for this reason,
when adequate support should have been provided. The people had
the ability, but owing to defective training, or lacking a proper concep-
tion of the nature of their obligations to their God and their pastor,
failed to help and encourage him as they should hove done.

The fault in these cases is not always or entirely with the people. The pastor sometimes rates himself above his worth. Or, perhaps, he has not "learned in whatsoever state he is to be content." He is not so ready as he should be to illustrate by his own example the graces of Pauline humility. The fact is, it require perceptions of a different order from those which many ministers possess, to enable them to see that they above all others should illustrate the beauties of saintly poverty.

The young pastor enters upon a field of labor which to him is new and untried. As he becomes acquainted with his work and his co-workers, he discovers influences operating which he believes would not only hinder his comfort, but his usefulness as well. With such a prospect before him, he at once determines to turn his face toward some other part of the great vineyard. It would have been well, perhaps, if he had somewhat curbed his youthful impulses. Still, it is better for a pastor to get away very suddenly from a charge, than to remain a long while after his usefulness in that field is at an end.

Another cause which not infrequently separates a pastor and his people is an invitation to another field—usually, as is supposed, a wider field of usefulness. Sometimes *this* "Macedonian cry" comes from a charge outside the pastor's own denomination. It does not seem to be thought now-a-days a matter at all indelicate to invite a pastor to leave his own charge and church. We all know that it would not be considered altogether civil to go around to your neighbor's back door, and propose to the kitchen-maid that if she would come to you she would find a *narrower* field of usefulness at much better wages. But while modern courtesy will not tolerate any interference with the relation existing between Bridget and her mistress, churches may cross not only denominational lines, but states, continents and seas to make overtures to a pastor, whom God hath joined in holiest relationship to a worthy and devoted people.

Again, many a pastorate, that at the beginning promised permanence, has been suddenly interrupted by "the springing up of some root of bitterness," which originated with some self-constituted leaders who did the pastor, as he thought, much injury. He entered upon his work with much earnestness, even enthusiasm. To him work for the Master seemed so reasonable, so befitting the Christian, so inspiring, that he wondered at the indifference he saw in some of his parishioners. And when at length the Alexanders and the Diotrepheses began to show their hand, the poor fellow's heart sank within him, his knees became feeble, and the complaint of Jeremiah voiced the feelings of his troubled soul: "Oh, that my head were waters and mine eyes a fountain of tears, that

I might weep day and night for the slain of the daughter of my people ! Oh, that I had in the wilderness a lodging place of wayfaring men ; that I might leave my people, and go from them ! for they be all adulterers, an assembly of treacherous men.'' The young pastor's eye falls upon another field ; it looks fair and promising. When we look at a forest from a distance, it seems to be made up of stately, noble oaks ; but when we get into it, there is an abundance of underbrush and gnarled scrubs growing right beside the grand oak. In every congregation there is some "wood, hay and stubble." There is, perhaps, as little in this as in any one you would find. Indeed, as I have looked upon this fold from my point of view, I have often during these twenty-five years agone, exclaimed with the son of Beor : "How goodly are thy tents, O Jacob, and thy tabernacles, O Israel ! As the gardens are they spread forth, as gardens by the river's side, as the trees of lign aloes which the Lord hath planted, and as cedar trees beside the waters.'' But doubtless even here as the eye of him, who walks amid the golden candlesticks, rests upon these trees of the Lord planted by Bruce, and Lee, and Reed, some are seen less stately than the cedar, less lofty than the palm !

In referring to some elements which give permanence to the pastorate I would particularly mention :

(1.) A consecrated minister. It is possible for a pastorate to continue for very many years, where the pastor is not remarkable for the possession of either natural or spiritual endowments. This may happen in a congregation largely made up of people of a low order of piety. The old proverb of the Prophet is still true, " Like people, like priest." A congregation greatly lacking in spirituality would not be suited with a minister who was devoted and faithful to his Master. An earnest pastor going into a congregation of "dry bones" will either produce a shaking among them, or he will soon be compelled to "shake the dust from his feet" and seek another field. Still, other things being equal, there is no more essential element to permanency than the piety of the minister.

The completely consecrated pastor will not be slothful ; will not dwadle away his precious hours in small talk among his parishioners, or in any other form of mental dissipation. He will follow Paul's advice to Timothy : "Give attendance to reading, to exhortation, to doctrine. Neglect not the gift that is in thee, which was given thee by prophecy, with the laying on of the hands of the Presbytery ; meditate on these things ; give thyself wholly to them ; that thy profiting may appear to all." Says Prof. Shedd, " The fact is that the holiest men in the Christian church have been the most studious men. Those spiritual and heavenly minded divines, who accomplished most in the ministry of their own day, and who have been the lights and guides of the ministry up to this time, were men of great learning. Augustine, Calvin, Owen, Baxter and Edwards were hard students. Henry, in his life of Calvin— a work which deserves to be read and pondered by every clergyman— furnishes striking examples of the studiousness of this great and intensely spiritual man. He was so assiduous in completing his Institutes, that he often passed whole nights without sleeping, and days without eating." One of the godly fathers of our own church, who still lingers amid the shadows of the border-land, at one time became so deeply interested in the study of a difficult portion of God's word, that for six days and nights he pursued the subject incessantly without taking a moment's sleep.

The conscientious minister will study carefully and closely in preparing for the pulpit from a sense obligation to his divine Master. He feels that he has a claim upon him for the very best that it is in his power to give. "Much study is a weariness of the flesh." But if we love and honor our Master as we should, like Paul we can say, "In weariness and painfulness, in watchings often, in hunger and thirst, in fastings often, in cold and nakedness."

That consecration, which produces diligence and earnestness in connection with the labors of the pulpit, will effect equal diligence and faithfulness in pastoral work. The minister who would do this part of his work well, so as to get from it the best results, must live near to his Savior ; must be deeply imbued with his spirit ; must have a heart to feel for others woes ; must be "a son of consolation." It is much easier to stand in the pulpit, and publish the glad tidings than to go from "house to house," comforting the smitten and afflicted, instructing the ignorant, guiding the erring, directing the inquiring, arousing the slothful, persuading the sinner, bowing at the bedside of the sick and dying, and there leading to a throne of grace a soul that must soon appear before the throne of glory. Often, often will the true pastor say with the Apostle, "Who is sufficient for these things?" Deeply will he feel his own insufficiency for work so solemn, work so closely connected with interests as enduring as eternity itself.

The pastoral work proper of the old pastor becomes in many cases doubly trying, because of the countless memories that come crowding into his mind and very soul, while every recollection brings a pang and every thought claims a tear. In that home where he ministers at the bedside of the dying youth, there, in other days, he talked and rejoiced, or wept and prayed with grandparents and parents ; tried to comfort them in trouble, and brighten their passage through the dark valley ; and now this dear one, whose early death will soon shadow the home, he baptized in infancy, admitted in early youth to the table of the Lord, and now sees him about to join the tearless, sinless generations that have gone before.

(2.)   Another element of permanency in the pastorate is a self sacrificing spirit on the part of both minister and people.   Selfishness and self-seeking by either pastor or people have led to the dissolution of many a pastoral relation.   In regard to salary, it would help much to perpetuate the relation, if pastors would be patient and forbearing to the extent of suffering loss and enduring hardship ; and if the people would be generous even to a fault in supporting their pastors.   In many cases the pastorate has been long, largely on account of the long suffering of the pastor.   The late Dr. Adams, of Madison Square Presbyterian Church, New York, gave in the course of his long pastorate some twenty thousand dollars for the priviledge of preaching to that wealthy congregation.   I could name an excellent minister of the same denomination, in this State, one of the longest settled pastors in the Synod, who recently said that he has not only spent all casual acquisitions, together with interest on private funds, but that he has sunk several thousand dollars of his patrimony ; and all this as pastor of one of the wealthy congregations of Western Pennsylvania !   We all know that pastorates are sometimes short because the pastor was inadequately supported, and sometimes they are long because he is inadequately supported, and says nothing about it !

But it is owing as often, perhaps, to the kind and generous spirit of congregations that pastorates are long.   Even good men and good ministers have their infirmities, just as Timothy had, and not a few of us have some that he did not have.   They do not uniformly preach neat, well arranged, fresh, juicy sermons.   He is a great deal better preacher and pastor than some of us are, if he does not often feel that his people are wonderfully patient and forbearing.   They do, as they should, make large allowance for our oft physical weaknesses, for our exhausting labors in visiting the sick, the sorrowful, the sinning, and for many, many other calls and distractions, which interfere with that close study and careful preparation which every faithful minister aims to give to his public discourses.   Christian forbearance on the part of both pastor and people is an important factor in giving peace and permanency to the pastorate.

(3.) Another element of long pastorates is the faithful preaching of the Gospel. A man may be what is called an entertaining and popular preacher; he may have a cultured and fashionable congregation, and they may remain together for a long time, even though the Gospel that is preached is a diluted Gospel or "another Gospel;" but such cases are exceptional. It is hoped that there not many congregations of this character in Evangelical Churches; and that there are few preachers suited to congregations that do not wish to hear sound doctrine. Paul exclaimed, "Woe is me if I preach not the Gospel;" and so will every true minister of Jesus exclaim; and the congregation that does not desire to have the Gospel preached to it, or is satisfied to sit year after year under a minister who does not preach the Gospel, is in a fair way to become, if it has not already become, as dead as the Church of Sardis.

If I were to philosophize in regard to the long pastorate we commemorate to-day and try to explain why it has continued so long, why it has been so happy and so productive of good, I would say that one reason, and the one that rises prominently in my mind is, that this pastor can say: "And I, brethren, when I came to you, came not with excellency of speech or of wisdom, declaring unto you the wisdom of God. For I determined not to know anything among you, save Jesus Christ and him crucified. And I was with you in weakness, and in fear, and in much trembling. And my speech and my preaching was not with enticing words of man's wisdom, but in demonstration of the Spirit and of power, that your faith should not stand in the wisdom of men but in the power of God."

There has been nothing of a sensational character in our good brother's preaching or methods. He has not sought to attract to his ministry those Athenians, who "spend their time in nothing else, but either to tell, or to hear some new thing."

He has not tried so to set his sails that he would be carried along by the breath of popular applause. No unworthy, no clap-trap methods have been employed to gather, or hold together, the congregation which for twenty-five long, eventful years have lived and labored together here in delightful peace and harmony.

We bless God for the proof we have to-day that those pastors who follow the methods of the Divine Master, of whom it was spoken: "He shall not strive, nor cry; neither shall any man hear his voice in the streets," are not left without encouragement, even though worldly wisdom would say, there are broader and better ways.

It encourages and strengtheus our faith in the power of the Gospel of Jesus Christ, when we see the plain, faithful preaching of that Gospel accomplishing successfully the work for which it was given to the world.

This pastor has for a quarter of a century sustained himself in this city, and what is better, has sustained the cause of Jesus; and yet he did " not strive, nor cry ;" did not shout as a warrior, or take up the cry of the demagogue; "his voice was not heard in the streets;" he believed that the pulpit, not the hustings, was the place where his voice should be heard ; and this long pastorate with its blessed fruits is pleasing testimony to the wisdom of his course.   That minister must have an ambition that is not born from above, who desires a wider and grander sphere in which to exercise his noblest powers than is given him in the great commission.   What higher, better, holier employmeut can he find, than to stand Sabbath after Sabbath before the people and declare with Paul : " Now then, we are ambassadors for Christ, as though God did beseech you by us ; we pray you in Christ's stead, be ye reconciled to God ?"   And what a pleasing retrospect does that pastor enjoy who can look back on a ministry of a quarter of a century or longer, and feel that all these years have been spent in preaching " the glorious Gospel of the blessed God ;" that he has preached it from the pulpit, preached it " from house to house," preached in season, out of season, and that his preaching has been owned of God " for the perfecting of the saints, for the edifying of the body of Christ."

How much longer this pastorate shall contiuue we know not.   Its future is only known to him who reads his own decrees.   But " the past at least is secure ;" its " witness is in heaven ;" its " record is on high ;" and pastor and people can say : With faith and hope we work and wait, "' till we all come in the unity of the faith and of the knowledge of the Son of God, unto a perfect man, unto the stature of the fullness of Christ."

After the congregation had sung Psalm 78 : 3-6, C. M., the Chairman said, I have the pleasure of introducing Dr. W. C. SHAW, of our own congregation.

THE SESSION.
BY WILLIAM C. SHAW, M. D.

It may be that originally the Committee of Arrangements, in appointing me to speak on this interesting occasion, had intended that some one theme should be subject of my discourse. No one yet spoken to on the subject has given me a very clear idea as to what is expected of me, more than that I am to represent the Session. Were it not for physical infirmity, the proper one to represent us would be our esteemed brother, Samuel George, our oldest member, and the only one who is now living, who has been continuously in the Session since the date of ordination and installation in May, 1851. He is also the only member of the present Session, who was a member twenty-five years ago.

Mr. John Herron, who was also ordained and installed at the same time as Mr. George, is still living and in good health, but is now connected with another branch of the church.

In keeping with the spirit of the occasion, which has called us together, as a Presbytery, Session, congregation and friends, to express our joy and thanks to our Heavenly Father, in leading us, as a pastor and people, through so many years, in love and peace, it will naturally follow that mention should be made of those who, with the pastor, constituted the Session of this congregation at the beginning of this quarter of a century, and those associated with him to the present time.

Having been connected with this congregation just one half the length of this pastorate, this task must necessarily be but imperfectly performed by me.

When Rev. W. J. Reid was ordained and installed, April 7, 1862, the members of the Session were, John Graham, Thomas Mitchell, Thomas Dickson, John Lowry, Samuel George, John Herron and George Rodgers.

The oldest member of the Session on April 7, 1862, according to the date of ordination, was John Graham, who was ordained and installed in the spring of 1832. He was not only a worthy member of this congregation, but was also favorbly known in the financial world, as President of the Bank of Pittsburgh, and he is still represented in that old, solid institution by its worthy cashier, William Roseburg, a nephew by marriage.   Mr. Graham died, Feb. 11, 1869, at the age of 75.

Next on the roll of that Session was Thomas Mitchell, who was ordained and installed, August, 1838.   Besides being a worthy member of this Session, he was widely known in the business community, having established a stove foundry in 1829.   Under different firm names, his name has been associated with that business till within a few years.   His good wife is still with us, and cheers us with her presence, when it is possible for her to attend services.   He died, April 1, 1871, aged 74.

Next on the roll was Thomas Dickson, who was ordained and installed, August, 1838,   He was for a time engaged in the grocery business, and finally settled on a farm at Swissvale, where he lived for many years, and where his family still reside.   I am told that he took sick in this church one Sabbath, and was carried to the residence of Mr. Thomas Mitchell, where he died, Feb. 16, 1870, at the age of 79, full of years, and of good faith.

The fourth member of this early Session was John Lowry.   He was for a number of years employed in the foundry of Mitchell, Herron & Co.; afterwards he was engaged as tax collector.   He lived an exemplary life, and died, Sept, 3, 1863, at the age of 79.

The fifth member was Samuel George, who was ordained and installed in May, 1851.   Mr. George was born near Newtownlimavady, Ireland, Dec. 15th, 1801.   He came to Baltimore in July, 1821, where he remained for two years.   In July, 1823, he came on foot to Washington County, Pa.   In January, 1824, he went into the grocery business in Pittsburgh with his brother Alexander.   At the death of his brother in 1840, Joseph Love, our beloved and lamented late treasurer, became a partner.   Mr. George has not been in active business for a number of years, and is now completely laid aside, by reason of the loss of sight, together with other infirmities of age, waiting for the call of the Master. Four of his brothers have held the office of ruling elder.

The sixth member of that Session was John Herron, who was ordained and installed in May, 1851.   He was engaged in the lumber business for many years.   He is still living at the ripe age of 81 years, and very active for his age.   He left this Session by certificate, Dec. 4, 1871, to unite with a neighboring congregation.

The seventh member was George Rodgers, who was ordained and installed in May, 1851.   He was engaged in the tobacco business for many years, but for some time lived a quiet and retired life, and died full of honor and of true faith, Dec. 10, 1880, at the age of 77.

These seven, with the pastor, constituted the Session of twenty-five years ago, but two of the seven now surviving, and they have reached the ripe ages of 86 and 81 years respectively, one of these now being a member of the present Session, but able no longer to meet with us. Of those who died, the youngest was 74, and two had reached the age of 79 years, showing a remarkable longevity.

It may be out of place in this connection, and in the presence of this assembly, but your historian wonders, whether or not these good men ever ate so much at the church sociables as do those of the present Session.

The first addition to the Session under this pastorate was, Oct. 20, 1864, when Messrs. Hugh McMaster and William Clendining were installed.

Most of you will remember Mr. Hugh McMaster as superintendent of our Sabbath School for many years. He was messenger for one of our city banks; was a quiet and modest man, and died, May 25, 1878, at the age of 58.

Mr. Clendining was engaged in the flour and grocery trade; was a humble, godly man, and died, January 11, 1878, aged 75.

The next election occurred early in 1872, when four new names were added to the roll.

First in order was William Douglas, who was installed, Feb. 1, 1872, having been a ruling elder previously in the Third United Presbyterian Church. He was engaged in the hat business, was a boy in vivacity all his life, and much esteemed by all who knew him. He died, Dec. 8, 1878, at the age of 76.

Next comes John B. Herron. I need not describe him, for every one knows him. He is another who never grows old in years, though what is left of his crown is whitened. He was ordained and installed, Feb. 1, 1872. He left this Session by certificate, March 16, 1880, to unite with the congregation of Noblestown. Returning to the city, he again united with this congregation, and is now a worshipper with us.

Next on our roll was George B. Millar, who was ordained and installed, Feb. 1, 1872. He was a clerk for James Wood & Co.; afterwards was engaged in the fire insurance business for a number of years. He died, May 29, 1877, aged 64.

The fourth of those installed, Feb. 1, 1872, was Prof. J. F. McClymonds, who was also ordained at that time. He was for a number of years principal of schools in one or other of our wards. Lately he forsook that field of labor for the green fields of Armstrong County, and left us by certificate, April 22, 1885.

We come now to the last addition to our Session, when six names were added to the roll, two by installation, having been ordained previously in other congregations, and four by ordination and installation. The date of ordination and installation of these six was Dec. 15, 1878.

Their names in alphabetical order as they appear on the roll are, William A. Edeburn, ordained and installed ; Thomas A. Elliott, ordained and installed ; S. L. McHenry, ordained and installed : James McMaster, installed ; William C. Shaw, ordained and installed.: J. G. Templeton, installed.

It is my painful duty to record the death of one of these. Mr. James McMaster, a gentle, kindly, good man, a perfect model of a Christian. He was engaged in the lumber business, was a contractor, was a director of a railroad, and of one of our banks. He meekly endured a painful affliction of body until God relieved him by death, July 30, 1882, aged 72.

We will leave to the future historian the task of recording the deeds of those of us who now survive, and are in active duty, hoping that our future service may be more efficient for the Master than has been our past.

The twenty-five years now ended have been years of peace and good will among us, and under God we owe much, very much, to the gentle spirit of him who has presided as Moderator over us, and whose counsel we were ever safe in following. We must also give the congregation due credit for seconding our will in any project undertaken by us.

We cannot boast of large increase in numbers, but we trust that when the great book of record is opened above, many names may be found enrolled there, of those whom we have recorded here on earth as belonging to this congregation.

THE CHAIRMAN.—Dr. J. G. TEMPLETON, a member of our own congregation, and Superintendent of our Sabbath School, will now favor us with an address.

THE SABBATH SCHOOL.

BY J. G. TEMPLETON, D. D. S.

It has been said that the children of to-day are the society, the church, and the nation of to-morrow. This, if not literally, is at least figuratively true. Those who shall succeed the active workers of to-day are now being taught, that they may take their places at the helm of church and state, and be the honored instruments in God's hand, in bringing the world to the haven of civilization and enlightenment under the influences of Christianity.

Having received from our ancestors the goodly heritage we now enjoy, it is our ever present duty to transmit the same to our successors, not only unimpaired, but with improved methods in accordance with the progress of the times in which we are called to act; and all without the least sacrifice of principle. To do our duty we must be progressive, and work in obedience to the injunction, " Whatsoever thy hand findeth to do, do it with thy might."

During the past twenty-five years, marvelous progress has been made in all departments of Sabbath School work. The methods and means of acquiring a knowledge of the Bible have been simplified and multiplied, and the cost of printed helps so reduced as to be within the reach of all. A quarter of a century ago the Chautauqua idea of instruction for the advancement of the Sabbath School cause was unknown to the world. Since its inception, practical methods have been demonstrated, the influence of which has extended to all evangelical denominations.

It was not until ten years after the establishment of the present pastorate, that the International System of Sabbath School lessons was adopted. In April, 1872, the National Sabbath School Convention met at Indianapolis, at which the chief subject of discussion was the propriety of attempting a plan of uniform lessons for the entire country.

In response to a popular demand in this direction, the leading Sabbath School publishers had agreed on a common schedule of Bible lessons for the year 1872. The experiment thus made was a success beyond the anticipations of those who arranged it.

The advantages of uniformity, and the ease of adapting the same portion of Scripture to all classes in the Sabbath School, were soon so apparent that the desire for a full series of common lessons spread rapidly throughout the country. The Indianapolis convention felt that there was an unmistakable pressure for a plan that should meet the popular want. The convention voted almost unanimously for the appointment of a committee of " five clergymen and five laymen to select a course of Bible lessons for a series of years not exceeding seven," which lessons should, so far as the committee might deem possible, "embrace a general study of the whole Bible, alternating between the Old and New Testaments." Out of the labors of that lesson committee, have gone forth influences for the impressing and uplifting of the membership of the church of Christ, such as have resulted from no other single movement since the days of the Reformation.

What example have we, and what authority is there given for the Sabbath School? We read in the 8th chapter of Nehemiah, that Ezra brought the Law before the congregation, both of men and women, and all that could hear with the understanding. We also read in this chapter the names of thirteen other teachers who assisted, and that they read distinctly, giving the sense, and causing the people to understand the reading.

The same authority, which uttered the ancient law—" These words which I command thee this day . . . . thou shalt teach diligently to thy children ;" re-enacted under the new dispensation. " Bring them up in the nurture and admonition of the Lord ;" also gave to his church the kindred law, " Feed my lambs." This double commission to the parent on the one hand and the church on the other, entrusting the religious instruction of the young not to *either* but to *both*, has never been repealed. It is too often neglected by the former, it has been too often overlooked by the latter.

It is the duty of the United Presbyterian Church to educate her young people. It was an Englishman who said, " If you would make anything out of a Scotchman, you must catch him while he is young." So if the United Presbyterian Church wishes to have well trained Sabbath School teachers, each congregation must organize its young people for normal class instruction, by which they can acquire such a knowledge of the whole Bible, as will qualify them for the position of teachers when their services are needed.

The Sabbath School service in the house of God is not a secular school in any sense. It is not a singing school, or a legitimate place for fairs and festivals, for tableaux, cheap theatricals and absurd dramatic performances.   It should not be a rostrum for itinerant Sabbath School talkers, or a place for pushing forward precocious children.   The Sabbath School is a department of the church, subordinate to and included in it as the greater includes the less, but it is at the same time one of the church's most important arms of service; and to be like Ezra's Bible class it should be composed of the whole congregation.

The Sabbath School should not be spoken of by the name of the Superintendent or any other officer or teacher connected with it, as his or her Sabbath School, but it is always proper to say our Sabbath School.

It is the duty of all church members to recognize their obligation to the Sabbath School, taking into consideration that the teachers give time in preparation, as well as time devoted to the exercises of the school on the Sabbath; also the valuable aid rendered to home instruction by a few kind words from the teacher commending the same.

We presume that every congregation would like have it said that their Sabbath School is a good one.

A good Sabbath School costs money, and the members of the congregation should feel that they are under obligation to give, and that it is worth all it costs; but it also costs what no money can buy, unselfish and tireless efforts of teachers.   No Sabbath School runs itself, unless it is running down hill, and then it cannot be called a good school.

"About the year 1840, a Sabbath School was organized in this congregation.   Before this time there had been union Sabbath Schools, sometimes in connection with the Associate Reformed congregation, and sometimes in connection with the Reformed Presbyterian congregation; but ever since a separate organization has been maintained."   When the present pastorate began, Mr. George Rodgers was Superintendent. He was succeeded by Messrs. Hugh McMaster, William Douglas, Thomas A. Elliott, William A. Edeburn and J. G. Templeton.

At the present time the officers of the school are, J. G. Templeton, Superintendent; Wm. A. Edeburn, 1st Assistant Superintendent; Jas. Loughridge, 2d Assistant Superintendent; G. Lambert Rodgers, Treasurer.

In addition to the Bible class taught by our pastor, Rev. Wm. J. Reid, D. D., there are three other Bible classes, which are taught by Miss Sarah Irvine, Miss Annie M. Adams and Mr. Robert W. Stewart.   The teachers of the intermediate classes are, Mr. S. L. McHenry, Mr. Robert McBride, Miss Sarah J. McIlwain, Mrs. T. F. Sturtevant, Miss J. L. Brownlee, Miss Maggie Duncan, Mrs. George B. Hill, Miss Lizzie McMillan, and Miss Mary J. McQuigg; Leader of singing, Mr. Harvey Littell.

The primary department is under the supervision of Mrs. Dr. Wm. J. Reid, and deserves more than a passing notice. It is no disparagement to any one connected with the school to say that the best work is being done in this grade. There are two methods of conducting primary classes ; the first is having all in one class, with one teacher. The second, or new method, is that in which the one having charge of the department takes the position of Principal or Superintendent, with several assistants, each assistant having a class of from five to eight pupils. Mrs. Reid has adopted the latter. And in language within the comprehension of the smallest scholars, the truths of the lesson are presented in a manner to attract their attention, and while they are listening to a story they are also learning the lesson. Every Sabbath, the previous lesson is reviewed with the connecting incidents; thus they are listening to a pleasant connected narrative ; and in after years the pupils thus taught will owe to these pleasant talks much of their knowledge of the Bible. After this they sing a selection from the Bible songs ; then each assistant teacher takes charge of her class and reviews the lesson. During the few minutes thus occupied, the Superintendent distributes lesson cards, papers, &c., and gathers the contributions, which for the year ending April 1, 1887, amounted to $125.00.

This amount was distributed among the different missionary enterprises under the care of the United Presbyterian Church, as follows: to Nile Boat, $44.00 ; to the Warm Spring Indians, $28.00 ; to the Little Girls' Home at Knoxville, $53.00; total, $125.00.

The teachers in the primary department are, Mrs. F. A. Stevenson, Mrs. Nancy Large, Mrs. Mary Bryce, Miss Jennie Thompson, Miss Maggie Martin, Miss Maria Moffat, Miss Della McHenry, Miss Hattie Creighton, Miss Hattie Creque, Mrs. Mary B. Reid, Superintendent.

The number of officers and teachers in the school is 27 ; the total enrollment 235, the contributions to the Boards of the church for the year ending April 1, 1887, $275.70; other donations, $20.00 ; total, $295.70.

A collection is taken up quarterly, on Communion Sabbaths, to defray the expenses of the school, which does not amount to what is required, the deficiency being supplied from the Session's fund. The money contributed by the school is used only to aid missionary enterprises.

After prayer, led by Rev. THOMAS W. YOUNG, pastor of the Fifth Church, the congregation united in singing Psalm 44: 1-4, 11s, when the afternoon session was concluded with the Benediction by the pastor.

The time from 5 to 7:30 o'clock was spent at the supper provided by the ladies of the congregation, and in social intercourse. About 700 persons sat down at the tables which had been spread in the basement of the church, and the former and the present members of the congregation found great enjoyment in recalling the incidents of the past.

EVENING SESSION.

The congregation sang Psalm 77: 5-10, C. M., and were led in prayer by Rev. W. J. ROBINSON, D. D., of the First Church of Allegheny, when the CHAIRMAN said, I have the pleasure of annoucing that Miss MARY O. LOW-RY, of our own congregation, will now read a paper.

WOMAN'S WORK IN THE CHURCH.

BY MISS MARY ORR LOWRY.

This is a subject which, from its importance, demands a great deal of attention. The church owes much of its influence to the quiet, persevering work of the women, who have been so greatly benefited by its doctrines. For there is no greater contrast between heathen nations and those under Christian influence, than the difference in the position of woman.

The importance of woman's work seems to have been recognized as early as the Apostolic era, though her sphere of action was somewhat restricted. If she were a widow, and not under forty years of age, she could have the office of deaconess conferred upon her. This gave her the privilege of assisting in preparing members of her own sex for baptism, and the right to administer consolation to those confined in prisons. Among her duties was that of sewing for the poor, for that good Dorcas for whom the rest of the widows wept, showing the garments she had made, was one of these widows or deaconesses.

I don't know why it was that in those early days a woman had to be a widow in order to take an active part in church work, unless—can it be possible?—that by making this arrangement the husband of that day received the undivided care and attention of his wife, without having to share either with the church.

But now and for many years since, all these restrictions have been removed, and any woman, no matter how lowly, be she maid, wife or widow, may serve that Master, publicly or privately, who in the moment of greatest agony had thought for the care and comfort of his earthly mother. And well have the mothers and daughters too, of these later days, heeded that Saviour's injunction with regard to the care of the poor and aged, whom we have with us always. Witness the homes for aged men and women, the homes and asylums for orphan children, and the industrial and mission schools throughout the city. These homes and schools, I know, are not kept up entirely by woman's work, but though the money for their support is not all earned by the women, it is so applied through woman's love and energy.

Dr. Gordon, in "Our India Mission," says, "When women undertake a good work, trusting in God—and they are more apt to trust him than are those of the stronger sex—they are pretty sure to succeed," and in nothing is this more clearly proven than in the work done by them in the Foreign Mission fields, particularly in India, where the women were kept in such close seclusion that it was almost impossible to reach them. They could not go out to hear the gospel, nor could the missionary carry it to their homes.

It seemed rather a dark outlook for these poor heathen mothers and through them for their children. But good women of our own, and other Christian countries, left home and friends to enter upon this work, a work which men could not accomplish. Girls' schools were established, but it required great patience and tact to get the girls to attend, for it is considered highly improper for girls, over eight years of age, to go upon the street unaccompanied. To overcome this difficulty some poor widows, whom custom allows to go about the street in search of food and employment, were hired to accompany the girls to and from school. The object of these schools was to teach the girls to read the Bible, and to bring them into contact with Christian influence in the school, that by this means the Bible might be brought into the Zanana or home. And in many instances this hope has been realized.

But time will not allow me to dwell at greater length upon this branch of the subject, as I wish to speak particularly of the work done by the women of our own congregation.

The first organized missionary work among the women of this church was begun during the pastorate of Dr. Bruce. At that time a society was formed, of which Mrs. Dr. Bruce was President, and Mrs. Young, Vice President. This society usually met at 'Squire Young's on Sixth avenue, as that was a central location, and by that means the expense of opening and heating the church was saved. The members subscribed fifty cents a year, and this, together with the money raised by any other means, was devoted to missionary work, home and foreign. The names of the members of this society, as far as I have been able to obtain them, are Mrs. Thos. Mitchell, Mrs. Love, Mrs. Alexander George, Mrs. Linton, Mrs. John Lowry, Mrs. Chambers, Mrs. Samuel George, Mrs. Boyd and Mrs. Roseburg. Of these, three are still living, namely, Mrs. Love, Mrs. Samuel George and Mrs. Mitchell, the latter being the grandmother of the president of the Young Women's Missionary Society of the present time. With these exceptions they have passed into the rest prepared for the people of God.

The next society was organized in 1851, when Mr. Lee was pastor of the church. It was known as the Female Benevolent Society. Article second of its Constitution reads, "The object of this society shall be to promote the cause of benevolence and appropriate the proceeds to whatever objects the society shall decide upon." This society met once a month at the home of some member, where the afternoon was spent in sewing. After a "plain tea"—the gentlemen being permitted to come in later—the evening was spent in social intercourse.

One of the first objects which received the attention of the society was the furnishing of the new church, that is, the one we now occupy. Pulpit furniture and carpets were considered sufficient furnishing in the old church, but these ladies decided, though not without some opposition, I believe, that cushions were necessary also ; so those upon which you are so comfortably seated were purchased with the money earned by their nimble fingers.

A society paper called "Light from a Dark Corner," was prepared and read at these monthly meetings. In looking over one of these old papers, I came across the following advertisement, which I have no doubt some of the bachelors of the present day would hasten to answer were the date eighty-seven instead of fifty-three : " With great pleasure we announce to the public generally, and the young and old bachelors particularly, that the Benevolent Sewing Society has, after much exertion, made arrangements to receive a few pupils to be instructed in the art and mystery of sewing on buttons, darning, etc. We feel confident that we shall receive the heartfelt thanks of our friends for this act of disinterested benevolence, as there are few who are ignorant of the deep anguish occasioned by the deplorable helplessness of single men in these departments of usefulness."

This disinterested benevolence did not seem to be appreciated as it deserved, for a little further on there is a poem commencing with these not very complimentary lines :

> " I really deem 'twould be as well
>   If in this vale of cares,
> Young ladies would just condescend
>   To mind their own affairs.
>
> 'Tis wonderful the constant bliss,
> .   Which little minds discover,
> In meddling with the ways and means
>   And doings of each other."

I may not be an impartial judge, but it seems to me that this advice is as applicable to one sex as the other.

With one more extract from a beautiful little poem entitled " Murmurs in the Grass," I will put the " Light" back into its " Dark Corner."

> " Hath thy murmurs aught of sorrow,
>   Where thy emerald waves are tossed,
> Crested all with foam white blossoms,
>   Art thou murmuring for the lost ?
> Many a stately ship lies shattered
>   Underneath the sounding seas ;
> But ' the grass ' upon the hillside
>   Waves o'er sadder wrecks than these."

The Women's Missionary Society of the present time was formed thirteen years ago, and was then known as the Ladies' Home Missionary Society, not receiving its present name until 1880. This society meets on the first Wednesday of every month, and although first organized as a sewing society, there is now no sewing done at the meetings. If there is some special case brought to its notice, such as preparing clothing for a poor family, or a box for some one under the Board of Ministerial Relief, the work is divided among the members and done at home.

During the last ten years, that is from 1877 till 1887, the society has raised $3,650, the receipts for the first year being $175 and for the last $618. Of this sum $1,813 has been devoted to Home Missions, $515 to Foreign Missions, $300 to the Quarter-Centennial Fund and $364 to the Oakland Chapel. A part of this money is obtained by having the members of the society furnish the supper for the monthly social, which is held in the lecture room of the church. Those who attend pay but twenty-five cents for their supper, and in so doing accomplish two good things. They replenish the treasury of the society and promote sociability among the members of the church.

Another means of raising money is by the envelope system, which was adopted by the society a few years ago. By this system each lady of the congregation who wishes it receives a package of twelve envelopes at the beginning of the year. On the first Sabbath of each month, she places a small sum varying from ten to twenty-five cents in one of these, and drops it into the missionary box at the church door. This contribution entitles her to membership in the society.

This society deserves a great deal of credit for the social, as well as the missionary work, done by its members. For nothing has done more to promote the pleasant, kindly relations among the members of this church than the social held under the auspices of this society.

Three years ago, through the influence of Mrs. Reid, our pastor's wife, a society was formed consisting of the young women of the congregation. The primary object of this society was to interest the young people in the missionary work of the church; to make of it a training school wherein the daughters would become accustomed to that difficult thing for the quiet home mothers—to speak out in meeting. You may think this of very little importance, but there you are mistaken; for sometimes a measure is carried through which is not at all adapted to the welfare of the many, simply because the many, whose opinion was quite as well worth hearing as that of the few who expressed theirs, were utterly unable to get up and express themselves clearly. Yet these same women, after the meeting has adjourned, can give their opinion without the least trouble. So you see the remedy for this evil is to have them begin the work so young that through practice it will become as easy to express themselves for the benefit of all as to give their opinion to their next neighbor.

Aside from this, the society is doing some excellent missionary work. There is a little Coptic girl in the mission school at Asyoot, Egypt, whose tuition it is paying, and when her education is completed, she will go out among the women of her country and tell them of the

Great Master, and of the religion that has done so much for the women of our land.

It has also charge of two rooms in the Orphans' Home, Allegheny. These rooms have been furnished throughout by the society, which has pledged itself to make all needed repairs with regard to carpets, furniture, etc.

During the three years of its existence, the society has raised $673. Of this sum, $150 have been used in educating the girl in Egypt, $130 for the Oakland Chapel, $214 for the Orphans' Home, $119 for small donations to different missionary causes, leaving a balance of $60 in the treasury at the present time.

One more society, and I shall have finished this record of the work done by the women of our church. This latest society consists of the members of the Sabbath School class taught by Miss Annie Adams, and was organized two months ago. The object of this society is to raise money enough to clothe a limited number of the mission children who attend our Sabbath School. The members meet twice a month at the home of some one of their number, where the time is spent in sewing. Orders for plain sewing are taken from the members of the congregation, and the proceeds are applied to the purchase of material to be used in their work.

May the members of these younger societies continue to work with such zeal and energy, that when the time comes that they will have to occupy the positions so ably filled by the members of the older societies, they will be able to do so with credit to the church and cause which they represent, deserving as many of those who have gone before the Master's meed of praise, "She hath done what she could."

After a vocal solo, by Miss JENNIE McKEE, the congregation listened to

FRIENDLY WORDS FROM OUR OWN PRESBYTERY.

By Rev. J. T. McCrory.

Personally I rejoice with you, pastor and people, on this happy occasion, and can only wish that the relationship formed twenty-five years ago may continue for at least another quarter of a century. I am sure, also, that the Presbytery on whose behalf I am to extend the friendly word of greeting is a unit in the same feeling and sentiment.

We all desire the continuance of this pastoral relationship, not for your sakes alone, but for ours also. As we are concerned for the good of the cause of Christ within our bounds, we are likewise concerned for the continuance of Dr. Reid in his present relation to this Presbytery. We have got right well acquainted with your pastor, brethren. He has been among us for a good while and has attended several meetings of the Presbytery—say a hundred more or less—and that would serve to introduce quite thoroughly a much smaller man than Dr. Reid. And then the doctor has a *weigh* with him that will not permit his presence to be overlooked or ignored; it is a *way*, we should say, of about two hundred and fifty pounds. That might be called a gross weigh, but it is not a bad way. It is such a jolly-good-humored-laugh-and-grow-fat way, that it has served to soften the Knox that are likely to be given and returned, where there are so many of us angular, poorly fed preachers. We all hope to copy this weigh of brother Reid when our salaries are increased. That is not the only reason, however, why brother Reid has been so fortunate as to attract the attention of Monongahela Presbytery.

The doctor has another way with him that we all have fallen in love with, and it is not at all a way of avoirdupoise either ; it is a way of doing more work for less pay and with a better grace than any man we wot of, and there is always a flattering recognition of such eminent talent and service in re-election to the offices of trust and—well let us stop with *trust*, for it is all trust—the Presbytery trusting the official with the care of all its important, burdensome, financial concerns, and the officer trusting the Presbytery in sums ranging from fifty to five hundred dollars, paid out of his own pocket on its account—mutual trust you see. Well, we trust that this state of mutual confidence shall continue for many years to come—until our debts are paid at least. We are glad to be able to bear testimony on behalf of our Presbytery, that your pastor stands first among the men faithful to every trust assumed by him on becoming a member of this body. However he may have discharged the solemn obligations of a minister of the gospel of Christ in other relations, there is but one opinion as to how he has conducted himself under his obligations to his Presbytery; and that opinion voices itself in the verdict that he has been a most faithful and efficient Presbyter. Indeed it has seemed to me that Paul's injunction in Rom. 12 : 11, "Not slothful in business; fervent in spirit; serving the Lord," must be Dr. Reid's motto in the performance of his Presbyterial duties. This suggestion is not intended as a mere compliment on this occasion of congratulation; we do not deal in empty compliments; but as a just recognition of the unflagging faithfulness with which an otherwise busy and burdened man has taken up and performed arduous duties without compensation at the call of his brethren. If Dr. Reid's service among us had had no other results than impressing, as it has done, the lessons of diligent attention to the duties of the high office of a Presbyter upon his younger brethren, we would be greatly his debtors. This lesson is one we all need to learn, all Christians, indeed; "Not slothful in business, fervent in spirit, serving the Lord." It is a lesson for the hour.

If time permitted nothing would suit me better than to take advantage of the opportunity offered to deliver you a brief homily on the text suggested. We would all do well to make it our motto in every relation of life; "Not slothful in business." And yet how many of us appreciate the value of time? Think of the duties laid on us by our Master, the work he has set us to accomplish, the shortness of the time given us in which to labor. And then think of the example of him who has called us into his royal service. He went about constantly doing good. And think, too, of the burning ardor with which he did his work and accomplished his mission. It made no difference what the particular duty was, he moved forward to its performance with the same zealous intrepidity, the same intensity of purpose, for it was all his Father's business; his Father's business, and so he moved as promptly and zealously to his work amid the bitter opposition and persecutions of Nazareth, as to the scene of his transfiguration on the Mount; his Father's business, and whether it was the ascent to Jerusalem, amid waving palms, heralded by hallelujahs of triumph from ten thousand throats, as "the king who cometh in the name of the Lord," or the ascent to Calvary, amid hootings and curses and cries of "Crucify him, crucify him," it was the same; there was no hesitation, no faltering, no want of purpose and zeal. Or if any one should think the example of the Master is too far beyond him, we might learn something worth remembering from the example of the author of this injunction. He has said, "Be ye followers of me, even as I also am of Christ."

No one, who reads Paul's history, will want a better commentary on this motto of his than the life of the great Apostle to the Gentiles. "Not slothful in business;" well, we should say not. If any man ever crowded a hundred years of labor into thirty-one years of life, that man was Paul, as we have his history between the taking up of his cross on his way to Damascus in A. D. 35, and the receiving of his crown at the hand of Jesus as he ascended from his martyrdom at Rome in A. D. 66. His fervency, also, was kept at a white heat from the beginning to the end of his grand ministry, while everything he did was with a single eye to the glory of God through Jesus Christ.

But this is a digression. It has served however, we trust, to emphasize our expression of the regard in which our brother is held by the members of his own Presbytery. It is too common to keep back all the good things we have to say of any one, until after he is dead, when if they don't do him any good, they won't do him any harm.

But Dr. Reid is old enough and big enough to stand the expression of the honest regard in which he is held by his brethren in Mononga-hela Presbytery. If any other member of the Presbytery should be called away, we feel that things would move right on without a jar; but if our big brother was taken from the family—well, let us not express an opinion, but hope that many, many years shall go by ere we are called, for any reason, to try the experiment. We rejoice with you in the prosperity of twenty-five years, and pray that God may give you many years of even more abundant prosperity together as pastor and people.

Rev. W. H. McMillan, D. D., of the Second Church,
of Allegheny, made the next address.

FRIENDLY WORDS FROM A SISTER PRES-
BYTERY.

By Rev. W. H. McMillan, D. D.

Mr. President.—It is my privilege to bring to you, on this great anniversary day, the greetings of the sister Presbytery across the river.
This is your day of proud retrospection and hopeful prospection, and
we, your neighbors in the field of Christian work, come to join your
songs of triumph, and mingle in your rejoicings.   It is right that we of
Allegheny Presbytery should join with you in celebrating this day, because we are interested in the success of this long pastorate, almost
equally with yourselves.   It is the duty of a Presbytery to teach the
truth of Christ, do his work, and defend his honor within its domain ;
but in doing these great duties, it receives much aid from the example
and influence of other Presbyteries, that are doing a like service for the
Master, along side of it.   Each division of the Lord's sacrameutal host
is helped in battling for the crown-rights of our King, by every other
division, that stands in the same line of battle; therefore the Presbytery
of Allegheny is made much braver and stronger for duty, by the near
presence of the grand old Presbytery of Monongahela; and as we of
Allegheny look across the river, upon the congregations and pastors
that compose this Presbytery, our allies in the service of Christ, we see
standing up in prominent strength and commanding influence the First
Church, with its pastor, who to-day stands crowned with the honor and
influence, derived from twenty-five years of faithful service.   If Dr.
Reid will pardon this personal reference, I will say what all will recog-
nise as true, that when a minister has held the position of pastor of an
influential church for a quarter of a century, he has proved himself to
be both able as a preacher of the gospel, and wise as an administrator
of affairs.   Changes have occurred in all the pastorates, except one, of
these two cities, since this one began, so that it stands now as the oldest
but one, of them all.   Some ministers who once stood in the pulpits
of these cities have been called away by death ; while they were holding
up Christ to the view of men, their own faces suddenly became trans-

figured by the vision of their Lord, and they passed upward out of sight ; some were separated from their flocks by the fitful changes of time ; some were compelled to surrender by reason of bodily weakness, and some, perhaps, by reason of their folly ; but amid all these changes, which the years have seen, this relation between pastor and people has only become closer, and more tenderly and strongly united.

The passing years have not produced decay here ; but rather, growth. What began as a union between two has grown into a oneness, and *relationship* has developed into vital *unity*. There is that which is especially sacred and beautiful in the relation between a pastor of many years, and the people who have grown up under his care. Dr. Reid remembers the time, when children, in the tenderness of infancy, were presented before him to receive the sacrament of baptism ; and he remembers too when those same children came, in the vigor and promise of their opening manhood and womanhood, to profess their faith in Christ, making good their parents' vows of former years, and showing him the fruit of his pastoral care ; and then that other day when they stood, with throbbing hearts, to plight their mutual troth, and be joined, heart and hand, for the long journey of life ; and, still on, his care has been over them ; in the days of adversity, when their burdens were heavy ; their times of sorrow, when their hearts were breaking ; as well as their seasons of joy, when life went well with them. Can we measure the strength of the ties thus formed ? or count the influence it gives him over his people ? Not long ago one of our official Boards offered Dr. Reid one of the most useful and honorable positions in our church, but a position that would have made a surrender of this relation necessary ; it did not require days, or even hours, for him to reach a decision ; his answer was given instantly : " No, I will stay with the First Church." Every pastor, who has been long enough in his place to feel the knitting of these ties, can understand why he so decided.

This influence of a long pastorate, *within* the church, is almost equaled also by the power it gives in the community at large. The paper, that published the anniversary sermon, said truly, that the sermon would be read with pleasure by multitudes, to whom Dr. Reid had come to be a well known, and revered minister of the gospel.

A man's public influence is undefined ; it cannot be described in words, or weighed exactly in the scales of our judgment, nevertheless we know it, and can feel its power. It is a thing of slow growth ; it is like a tree, it cannot be manufactured in a hurry, it must develop little by little ; but, when once acquired, it is a power of good, that only God can measure. There is a potency going out from such a pastorate

as this, upon the community round about, in favor of truth and righteousness, rebuking wrong, and leading toward God, which reaches
further and acts with more force than we will ever know. We can see
something of the injury that is done, when a minister of Christ goes
down in sin and shame ; and is not that the counterpart of the good,
produced on the public mind, when an embassador of Christ has proved-
himself true and faithful ?   In the achievements, therefore, of this long
pastorate within the parish, and in its results without, we find reasons
for bringing to you our congratulations to-day.

There are special reasons, also, why I should come to you with words
of friendly greeting to-day.   I have the honor to be pastor of a church
that is a child of this one.   On the 26th of October, 1837, Dr. Bruce,
then the pastor of this church, organized what is now the Second United Presbyterian Church of Allegheny, with Wm. Bell and John Chambers as its first elders, who had both served in that office here, and went
out, together with a number of members from this flock, to form the
new organization over the river.   Next October we will invite our parent church, both pastor and people, to come over and celebrate with
us our fiftieth anniversary as a congregation.   You see then that there
are special reasons why I should take pleasure in bringing this message
of greeting, for I come, not only as representing a sister Presbytery,
but as the pastor of a church which is the offspring of your own.

And now what lies beyond this silver wedding?   Our prayer is, that
the years may stretch on and on to the *golden* wedding, in unbroken
peace, and ever increased prosperity.   Your pastor has promised you
that he will still preach the same gospel, and that is what you need ;
you are sure, that he will be to you the same pastor as before, with ever
more and more of paternal wisdom and love ; he will be with you still
on your joyous *fete* days, when, amid the strains of the wedding march,
and the sweetness of orange blossoms, you hear the silver hammer fall
that shall weld two happy hearts into one ; and he will come to you
when the crape hangs at the door, and your life is *so* dark and lonely :
if there is one of you discouraged, your pastor will still grasp him by
the hand and hold him up ; if one is going astray, he will follow him
with warnings ; if any of the flock are sick, you will still see him kneel-
ing beside the sufferers.   Thus the under shepherd and his flock will
move on together toward the evening time, when all shall rest safely in
the fold above.

Anniversaries are strongly suggestive of eternity.   Looking back at
the way we have come leads us naturally to ask, how far it may be to
the end.   How swiftly the years are running by !   But this is not a rea-

son for sorrow; it is another cause for congratulation. The people of God do not fear the future; they are pressing toward it with delight.

> " We are dropping down the noisy river
> To our peaceful, peaceful home,
> Dropping down the turbid river,
> Earth's bustling, crowded river,
> To our safe eternal home,
> Where the rough roar riseth never,
> And the vexings cannot come;
> O loved and longed for home ! "

THE CHAIRMAN.—With more than ordinary pleasure, I announce that the next address will be by Rev. WILLIAM McKIBBIN, pastor of the Second Presbyterian Church of this city.

FRIENDLY WORDS FROM A SISTER CHURCH.

By Rev. WILLIAM McKIBBIN.

Honored Sir and Brethren of the First United Presbyterian Church of Pittsburgh:—It gives me great pleasure to stand here and bear to you my hearty congratulations, upon your completion of the quarto-centennial of your relationship as pastor and people. And in so doing, I feel that I am representing not only my own sentiments, but those of the great Christian community in these cities outside of your immediate ecclesiastical lines. We feel that this church and its pastor have been a power for the furtherance of the gospel, and belong to the entire church of Christ in this region. While loyal to its own distinctive denominational positions, it has recognized the law of moral perspective, and made Christ and his Cross the central figure and fact in its teaching, not permitting subordinate matters to eclipse essential ones, and questions of church life and administration to push into the background the great Head of the Church. But an uninterrupted and successful pastoral relation, extending over a quarter of a century, is a matter for congratulation, not only because of the pleasure which the continuance of such a tie must increasingly impart, but because of the admirable qualities which it discloses both in pastor and people.

Such a prolonged relationship stamps the pastor as a *wise* man. No one could have carried forward successfully, for twenty-five years, the multiplied activities and the varied development of so complex and delicate an organism as a church, in a community which has undergone so many changes as this, and amid the conflicts of modern thought and life, unless he had been a wise man. These changes have been at once so powerful and universal as to have extinguished some and seriously crippled many of the strong churches in all ecclesiastical folds.

Such a pastorate assures us that Dr. Reid is a *patient* and *peace-loving* man. I do not mean to intimate that the history or circumstances of this congregation have called, in any special degree, for the manifestation of such a spirit; but all congregations pass through periods in their history, when peculiar opportunities and temptations are presented to pastors to do or to say imprudent things, and alas! many avail themselves of these occasions. In such crises, patient waiting and working, coupled with a strong love for the things which make for peace, are of inestimable value. Such crises are marks often of a church's growth. A church without friction is apt to be one without life, and a very tame affair. It is said that Dr. Chalmers was, upon one occasion, visiting a pious cobbler, a member of his congregation, who in the course of the visit expatiated at some length upon the happiness of his wedded life, capping the climax with the statement: "Me and me wife, doctor, have lived together for forty years and never had a word." The old doctor gruffly replied: "Mighty monotonous, mighty monotonous." So a church life without occasional heat and friction would be "mighty monotonous." But at such times it requires the patient and pacific pastor to allay irritation and guide into safe channels the energy, whose liberation is often marked by a rise in temperature.

The successful completion of this twenty-five year pastorate marks Dr. Reid as a *growing* man. No man could hold the congregation together and build them in grace and knowledge of Christ, unless he himself had been a growing man. This last quarter of a century has been filled full of new thought, new developments, new problems. The unchangable gospel has been called upon to meet new conditions and face new questions, and unless the pastor of this church had been a growing man he would have been outgrown.

He has been an earnest student, these twenty-five years, of the Word of God, of the human heart and of the thoughts of the wise and good who have sought to unfold the meaning of God's Book and apply its healing virtue to sinful and sorrowful humanity.

Much has been said about the disadvantage which age brings to a minister. Some seem to feel like the old preacher who said he was born at the wrong time; that when he was young old men were all the go, and when he was old young men were all the go. Growing men are never outgrown, and if there is a ministerial "dead-line," it is apt to be, as some one has said, the "lazy line." I congratulate your pastor upon having, by faithful study, continued during these years to meet the growing demands of a growing church, in a growing community, amid growing obstacles. Dr. Reid evidently has not turned his "barrel" over very often.

I further congratulate him that he has preached the gospel during these years. Nothing but the gospel could have held this church together and sustained so vigorous spiritual life for a quarter of a century. It is a blessed testimony, in this novelty loving age, to the permanent attractive power of the gospel. "And I, if I be lifted up from the earth, will draw all men unto me."

Men may heed the message or reject it, but it will compel attention; ever new, ever old, like the glorious lights and shades of the skies: endless variety in unchangable unity. I congratulate your pastor that, amid the conscious infirmities and imperfections of these past years, he can honestly say that he has endeavored to pour, into the foul pool of this great city's life, the pure, healing waters of that "fountain, opened to the house of David and to the inhabitants of Jerusalem, for sin and uncleanness."

But I congratulate your pastor upon the *Christian Catholicity* which he has shown during these years. In those great fields of effort, religious, philanthropic and educational, which call for undenominational co-operation among the various cohorts of the church of Christ, he has ever been found in the foremost rank and doing the hardest work. As the chosen teacher of the teachers of the Sabbath schools of our cities, he has found, in the hearts of the Christian workers of our churches, a position which is *facile princeps*. We, as Christians of every name, must rejoice in the spiritual prosperity which you have enjoyed because we have been large sharers in its blessing.

But I must congratulate this church upon having made Dr. Reid the man he is. I use the word "made" advisably. Few realize how much churches can do to make or unmake their ministers. While every man has his own strongly marked characteristics, yet which of them shall be developed, and in what proportion, is largely determined by his environment. You have given to your pastor an environment which has stimulated and drawn out those qualities which have made these years so fruitful. Acting and reacting upon each other, you are both the creations of each other. You have stood by him in his good work. It is not every church that knows when it has a pastor to whom it ought to stick; you seem to have known that fact. You have honored his faithfulness, have received the truth at his hands loyally and lovingly. You have not asked him to shrink his declaration of the whole counsel of God, so as to leave your weaknesses and sins unchallenged. You have been ready imitators and helpers of his broad, Christian charity. In all good works, within and without your own denomination, you have sustained him, and the names of your members find honorable mention in all the Christian enterprises of our communities.

Standing by your Ebenezer here to-day, as a Christian man and a Christian minister, representing, I believe, the entire Christian community, I bid you God-speed for another quarter of a century. The cause of Christ in this region needs this church and its pastor, and in loyalty to the Great Head of the Church, we rejoice and will rejoice in your strength and prosperity, because it comes from him and is dedicated to him.

A duet was then sung by Miss JENNIE McKEE and A. W. RAMSEY.

THE CHAIRMAN.— The next address will be made by an eminent United Presbyterian, one whose name and fame are known to all Evangelical Churches. Although he is affectionately regarded as one of the fathers of our Church, his appearance and his voice give no sign of old age or of abated strength, but rather of the power and elasticity of the prime of vigorous manhood. As a fitting close to this festival of speech and song, his words will crown the entertainment with "apples of gold in pictures of silver." I have the honor of introducing Rev. Dr. DAVID R. KERR.

Dr. KERR, (Editor of the *United Presbyterian*, and Professor in the Allegheny Theological Seminary,) spoke as follows :

LET BROTHERLY LOVE CONTINUE.

By Rev. David R. Kerr, D. D., LL. D.

There may be more of the essence of religion in obedience to the first table of the law, that which prescribes our duty to God, but there is more of the evidence of it in the obedience required by the second table, that which prescribes our duty to man. It is, at least, more open to human observation.

The soul of the obedience in either case is love ; in the one case love to God, in the other love to man. Or, as the Saviour sums the commandments: " Thou shalt love the Lord thy God with all thy heart, and with all thy soul, and with all thy strength, and with all thy mind ; and thy neighbor as thyself." That is the law for humanity at large. But there is a brotherhood of men, a closer and more sacred one, in which love is still more binding, more tenderly, strongly binding, than in any mere natural relations, or under any mere legal requirements. It is the brotherly love binding together those united to Christ by faith, and who through him have become members of that family of which God is the father and Christ the elder brother.

It is of the workings of love in this brotherhood, Paul writes so glowingly in the thirteenth chapter of his first epistle to the Corinthians. It is true the original term he uses means more than that into which it is translated in our received version—more than *charity* in its commonly accepted sense. It includes love in all its workings towards God and towards man. But from the representations of it given by the Apostle, it is evident he had chiefly in view the love of the brethren. It is the love that suffereth long and is kind—that envieth not—that boasteth not itself—that is not easily provoked, thinketh no evil—rejoiceth not in iniquity, but rejoiceth in the truth—beareth all things, believeth all things, hopeth all things, endureth all things—the greatest of all Christian virtues—greater than faith or hope. The same Apostle, writing to the Romans, enjoins on them to be of the same mind one toward another—to the Ephesians, to be kind one to another, tender hearted, forgiving one another as God for Christ's sake had forgiven them—to the Hebrews, that while holding fast their profession without wavering, they should consider one another, to provoke unto love and good works. Such declarations of the workings of brotherly love give us the Apostolic ideal of it.

If all God's people had it, we would not have his church divided into so many denominations with their differing creeds and orders of government and worship. If all his people of any one denomination had it, we would not see in it so many divisive courses, brethren making offenses against each other, magnifying differences and wasting energies and resources in useless and often bitter strife. If every congregation of God's people had it, there would be a peace and joy in the fellowship of its members and a hearty co-operation in all its work, that would lift it far above any present experience.

In its perfection it does not now exist. There is too much of the militant in this imperfect state for that. But the Apostolic ideal of it remains, and this all Christians in all congregations should seek to reach. Some congregations are much nearer it than others. I am here to-night to congratulate this congregation on an exceptional enjoyment of brotherly love, and to make a plea for its continuance. This claim for you is abundantly sustained by the demonstration of this day. That you have had like distinction in the past we have as good reason to believe. I cannot recall the beginnings of your history as covered by the first pastorate, the short one of Henderson; nor the early years of that of his illustrious successor, Dr. Robert Bruce. But the latter it was my privilege to know in the closing years of his ministry among you, and more closely as one of his students in the old University of which he was then Principal. Knowing him as I did, and loving him as all his students did, I can readily conceive how a congregation with such a pastor would become bound to him and each other in the warmest bonds of brotherly love. He could scarcely have been more esteemed by you than he was in all this community, in which he stood so eminent, not only for learning, but for loveliness of Christian character. The congregation would be half heartless that, under such a pastor, would not be united in grateful enjoyment of love to him and each other.

After him you had the two years' pastorate of the beloved Anderson, and then the five years' one of the equally beloved Lee, whose services you so highly appreciated, and under whom you had not only great prosperity, but the delights of brotherly love. The few years between that time and the settlement of your present pastor do not appear so bright. You had the service of a good man in S. B. Reed, and a good preacher, but different in some things from his predecessors, and on that account, perhaps as much as anything else, disappointing to some of the congregation. The result was the dissolution of the pastoral relation at the end of two years. In itself it may have been an adversity, but it was overruled for good. It gave us a new church, our present Fifth. through which so much good has been done, and left you in a condition in which you have gone on in peace and prosperity, increased and increasing, all the years since.

Whatever darkness may have appeared then, or at any other time in your history, has been swallowed up in the general brightness. Any troubles you may have had, so far as they can now be recalled, at most, are but as spots on the sun. In the retrospect of this hour, the visions that rise before us are of a church which, through all the vicissitudes of her history, has been preserved and prospered, blessed and made a blessing—a mother church, constantly sending out her benign influences all around her, and often her godly members to establish and build up other churches—all the time holding her own place in the front, and holding it grandly, amid all the adverse influences of a shifting population and floods of inflowing wickedness.

And the line of ministerial service that comes down, like a thread of silver, through your past history, how brightly it glows this evening as it connects with that of your present pastor! What shall I say of him? What need I say more than has been said of him by our president and others who have spoken? I will rather speak of the delight I have had in hearing him so praised. I have more reason for this than you may think; and, also, to take some honor to myself here. You would scarcely think, in looking at the portly form and hoary head of your pastor, that he was one of my boys—one, at least, whom I had a part in training for your service. I tell you, it gives me great pleasure to see the proportions into which he has grown among you—I am not speaking of his body now—but of his mind and heart, and whatever else goes to make up a well-rounded character and useful life.

But you do not need anything from me to help your appreciation of him. You know him well, and it is but natural that in your love of him you should have the brotherly love among yourselves, of which this celebration is but an ardent expression. What I am to urge on you is the continuance of this love.

I urge it for its own sake, as one of the most beautiful exemplifications of Christian character and Christian living, that even worldlings in looking on you may be constrained to say: See how these Christians love one another.

I urge it for your pastor's sake, that the remaining years of his ministry among you may be cheered by the continued unity and harmony of his people, and their hearty co-operation with him in all good works.

I urge it for your own sakes—for the comfort you will have in it— the profit as well as pleasure it will give you—that bound together in bonds of love, you may have the unity that will make all your associations and all your work as members of the same congregation a continued delight.

I urge it for the sake of the work you have to do. You will need it for efficiency in all your work at home and abroad, and, if for nothing else, in maintaining yourselves as a congregation in the part of the city in which you are placed. The growth of business and the enlargement of business facilities, so rapidly taking possession of the old parts of the city, are as rapidly driving the old population into the outlying districts. Those who remain and those coming in with the tide of trade are largely of a class difficult to reach by church influence. But they have souls, and they need salvation. And here they are in the whirl of a demoralized city life. You are one of the churches God has kept in the midst of them. The work demanded will require your undivided strength. Let it have your united hearts and united energies; and that it may have, cultivate and continue the brotherly love that has given you so much of your past and present power and prosperity.

With the same power preserved you may have a future in which you will be still more blessed, and more of a blessing to others. God grant it, and richly endow you all, pastor and people, with all the blessings of his grace.

The Mendelsohn Club sang a quartette, when the Chairman said :

PRESENTATION ADDRESS.

BY THE CHAIRMAN.

I am compelled to interrupt the exercises, prescribed by the programme, to perform a duty suddenly devolving upon me. The worthy Treasurer of our congregation handed to me an envelope containing a check, which represents what may be appropriately designated a " Conscience Fund." I understand that it represents a considerable sum of money. Now, our popular Treasurer has been in office longer than a decade, and he has been a trusted and faithful officer.

Although we never put him under bonds, he has not misapplied any of the large sums that he has handled, and is continually controlling. Yet we took "a bond on fate," and fully protected our trust, by a novel process; we always kept the congregation in his debt, and we felt sure that he would not go to Canada while we were indebted to him! He assures me, however, that he is not restoring any gains made through his office, but that the money represented by this check came recently from the members of the congregation, both women and men; that the retrospect produced by this celebration, and quickened consciences, or a more tender element of their character, induced the members to bring to him, voluntarily, numerous sums of money, which they all requested should be given to our pastor, as a substantial and tangible testimonial of their thankful hearts! We all join in this material expression of good will. We do not offer it in discharge of our obligations to you, sir; (addressing Dr. Reid,) we cannot pay our debt of gratitude; we cannot measure, by any earthly measure, the height or breadth or depth of our love for you; we cannot express by any gift, though it were thousands of times greater than this, the fulness of our confidence, the strength of our affection, or the depth of our gratitude! We only desire to exhibit in this moment of supreme pleasure, that our hearts would do more than express our emotions in speech and song! We only regret that this token of good will is not greater, and more worthy of the man and the occasion. But we give it not to you alone. It is tendered to you and your honored wife, and for the use and benefit of both. We would not forget her in this hour of congratulation and happiness. The love of this congregation goes out to her from our hearts, as strongly and tenderly as it reaches the tendrils of your heart. We respect and love her for her virtues, her faith, and her work.

We know, sir, that you are an abler and a greater man and minister because she shared your labor and perplexities, as well as your love, for nearly a quarter of a century. She has been indeed a help-meet to you in all your work, a partner of your purposes and of your hopes. Her heart and hand and brain have worked lovingly, intelligently, and faithfully to promote the prosperity and success of our Church, and no pastor's wife could have been more willing, faithful, and successful in performing the duties, both public and private, of her position. She has been sunshine for the sorrowing and a blessing for the mourning. Her work in the Sabbath School has greatly tended to the sanctifying and blessing of our homes through the training of our children, and her gentle Christian heart has given tone and character to woman's work in our church.

I am instructed to say, also, that at a very recent congregational meeting, you were granted a six months' vacation, to be taken within the present year, at your own discretion and convenience ; and this for the purpose of enabling you and your good wife to gather fresh strength for the coming years of your work here.   You have worked too hard ; more than man should do, and we want to give you needed rest.   We don't want to get rid of you.   On the contrary, we will miss you, and be impatient for your return ; but we make this sacrifice in the belief that that you need rest, and that you will return to us with renewed physical strength to do the duties of the next quarter of a century; for we sincerely hope and pray that your life may be spared to us for long years to come.

Accept our gift, then, freighted with the love of many hearts, to yourself and to your true and good wife.

A word more.   We know your broad charity and unbounded liberality.   You give, and give continually, to every worthy object, and in the fulness of your beneficence, you do injustice to none but self.   Don't give this money to the Monongahela Presbytery or any other more or less worthy object.   Keep and use it for the single purpose for which it has been provided.

The Chairman then introduced H. KIRKE PORTER, as the representative of the Young Men's Christian Association of Pittsburgh, who presented Dr. REID with the greeting of the Association he represented, and with a watch and chain.

GREETINGS OF THE YOUNG MEN'S CHRISTIAN ASSOCIATION.

BY H. K. PORTER.

MR. CHAIRMAN AND FRIENDS:—It is an Apostolic injunction to re-joice with them that do rejoice. On this occasion of joy in your church home, it is a delight for your friends to come and join in your festivities.

Words of friendly greeting have however been already spoken by those from without the family circle, and my words might be spared; but I am charged with a special service by many to whom Dr. Reid has rendered a service of special value.

The Young Men's Christian Association of Pittsburgh, an organization representative of all Evangelical churches, has been in active operation during more than twenty years of your pastor's ministry. Earnestly has he assisted that body, in many ways, when we have called upon him. But in its rooms, and now in its own building, a still wider company of Christian men and women have been gathered weekly for the study of the Word. Dr. Reid, for now the full period of ten years, has been the teacher of this band of teachers. You, who know so well how fitted he is for this important service, will know and appreciate the feelings of esteem, and regard, and affection, which we have come to cherish toward him.

We are only too grateful to your committee, Mr. Chairman, for having so hospitably extended an invitation to us to come, and by our presence to express these feelings, and have been only too glad to bring a lasting memento to remain as our witness, and now in this moment of the culmination of your joy, you permit us room and voice. I count it a special honor, and could only wish that I might convey to Dr. Reid, and to you all, our sense of indebtedness and of cordial admiration.

For one, I rejoice at the pronounced and unmistakable character of his teachings. These have been with no uncertain sound. To him, the law of the Lord has been, and has been shown by him to be, perfect; the testimony of the Lord has been, and he has never doubted it, sure: the statutes of the Lord, right; the commandment of the Lord, pure; the fear of the Lord, clean; the judgments of the Lord, true and righteous altogether: more to be desired than gold, yea than much fine gold; sweeter also than honey, and the honey comb. And while teaching this word of his Lord with all fidelity and plainness, he has done it with such cheer that his very method has been an inspiration. How wide the influence for good thus exerted has been, and how great it is, is beyond all human computation. At that time when the secrets of the deep are given up, and the hearts of men are laid bare, the fruit of this sowing shall be known.

These hundreds of teachers, representing at least one hundred of our Sabbath Schools, have charged me by their representatives to come to you, our revered teacher, on this day of joyful reminiscence, to bear to you their warm congratulations, and their earnest, loving prayers for continued and increasing blessing on all your work. They delight as well to bring you a gift that they trust may prove useful and a pleasure ; and in the selection of this watch and chain, they have had the thought that oftentimes it would carry with it a reminder of them. With sympathy and deep interest in the work that the Great Teacher of us all permits you to do for him in our community, and in the broad domain of his kingdom, they go with you in spirit ; and if this shall be the message that our token shall bring to your heart, it will have served its purpose.

In response to these gifts and greetings, the pastor said :

MR. CHAIRMAN AND FRIENDS:—My heart has been full to overflowing all day. I cannot trust myself to respond to these testimonials and greetings. But there is a gentleman in the audience, who has always stood by me as a boy, as a man and as a minister, and I am sure that he will help me now in this, one of the most embarrassing hours of my life. I can only say, I thank you ; and I would call on Dr. W. J. ROBINSON, pastor of the First Church of Allegheny, to speak in my behalf.

Dr. Robinson, in compliance with this request, spoke as follows :

RESPONSE FOR THE PASTOR.

By Rev. W. J. Robinson, D. D.

Mr. Chairman, and Gentlemen of the Young Men's Christian Association:—Dr. Reid asks me to respond for him on this interesting occasion, on the ground of a lifelong friendship. I may be permitted to explain at the outset of my remarks, that a good many years ago, when we were boys together, in the fervor of a youthful affection and confidence, we entered into a kind of co-partnership for life, agreeing to "pool" our individual gifts, and attainments, and hold them in common. The mutual contribution of stock to the concern was not exactly equal. It was very much like that of the small boy with his older brother. "Me and Tom," said the little fellow to his companion, with a good deal of pride, "have fifty cows." "Fifty cows!" exclaimed his companion, with admiring surprise. "And do you own twenty-five?" "N-n-no," said the boy, "it's not exactly that way. Tom has forty-nine and I have one." That about expresses the relative value of my stock in our company. When referring to this co-partnership, I am compelled to put the word "Limited" over my signature. One of the stipulations of the agreement was that he was to receive his music from me, and I was to receive my theology from him. And this accounts for the fact that the congregations are saddest when he sings, and when I preach. Now I suppose it is because of this co-partnership between us that I am asked to perform this very pleasant service for the Doctor to-night, and because my share in it is so limited, I feel that I can speak very freely.

And I am sure I may say that these graceful testimonials are accepted by him to whom they are tendered, not only for their intrinsic value, but especially for the sentiment which they convey. Because they express an affection, a confidence, a high esteem on the part of a great host of friends in this community ; because they are the sweet incense of loving hearts laid upon the altar of a long and tried and cherished friendship, these kindly tokens have a priceless value in his sight. Next to those soul-uplifting assurances of the *Divine* favor and accept-

ance, which come to the faithful Christian in favored moments and at
rare intervals, are just such assurances as these which you have given
to-night of the loving confidence and esteem of earthly friends.   And
they are peculiarly precious to the Christian minister.   From the very
nature of his office and work among men, forbidden as he is to consult
their pleasure or to pander to their tastes, or to seek honor from men,
and yet in no small degree dependent for success as well as comfort in
his work upon the affection and confidence of those to whom he ministers, such testimonials to him rise to a higher plane than that of mere
personal consideration.   They become assurances of Divine acceptance
in his high and holy office.   " Ye did well," writes the great Apostle
to his beloved friends at Philippi, acknowledging a similar remembrance
by them, "that ye did communicate with me.   Not that I desire a
gift, but I desire fruit that may abound to your account."   Because
their gift carried with it the assurance to his heart that his labor was
not in vain among them, it was peculiarly acceptable to the great
Apostle.   And I think I mistake not when I say, that these testimonials
have their chief value to the recipient in the fact that they have similar
intent and meaning.   They are accepted by him as expressing, first,
your high appreciation of the great controlling purpose and aim of his
twenty-five years' ministry among you.   Reared in a school of Christian
thought, which gives a high place to the Christian ministry, imposes
upon it a high obligation, holds it to a responsibility above every other
calling, regards it in the highest sense a ministry of God for good to
man, Dr. Reid came among you twenty-five years ago with no ordinary purpose in his mind.   He set up before himself a high standard
of ministerial obligation.   He consecrated the dew of his early manhood to a lofty service.   And through all these years he has held himself to the one effort of attaining his ideal.   He has made it his aim to
be an able minister of Jesus Christ ; to preach Christ and him crucified ;
to unfold the great saving doctrines which centre in the cross ; to
expound the truths of this blessed word with clearness, simplicity and
fidelity ; to declare the whole counsel of God.   He has never been
willing to prostitute his high office, or lend his gifts to mere secular
ends.   He has scorned the thought of converting his pulpit into a
stage for mere acting.   He has never allowed himself to yield to the
demand, so great at the present day, for a mere sensational pulpit.   He
has known too well the worthlessness of such service.   He has already
outlived five or six dispensations of the gospel of sensation in this city.
Let the Jew demand a sign, and the Greek seek after wisdom ; he has
aimed to preach Christ crucified, the power of God and the wisdom

of God. This, it can be truly said, has been the controlling aim of his ministry of a quarter of a century among you. And with this, there has been a controlling desire and purpose to be a true servant of his fellow men. He has desired, and aimed to be among you, like his Master, "as one that served." He has aimed to be ready for every good work, to respond to every legitimate call upon his time, and talents, and energy, to enter every door of service which his Master might open to him : while faithful to his own people, to have his ear open to the cry for help from whatever quarter it might come. This has been his controlling aim and purpose, and he accepts with grateful emotions these proofs which you have given him to-night that this great community has caught the true purpose of his aim—has interpreted it aright, and has set a high estimate upon it.

And, second, he accepts these testimonials as an expression of your high appreciation of the spirit, in which he has lived and done his work among you : a spirit of kindness, loving sympathy, good will and great good nature. As every one knows, Dr. Reid has been richly endowed both by nature and grace with the attractive graces of kindness and good humor. It is *natural* for him to laugh, and he knows how to make others laugh. He has an eye to see and a soul to enjoy the bright and cheery, and even the ludicrous things in life. There is a tradition that when he first opened his eyes upon this queer world, and saw the old homestead, and the grave faces round about him, and found that he had come to stay awhile, he laughed outright at the very joke of the thing. The tradition may not be wholly reliable. But that Dr. Reid is able to extract more real juicy sweetness from the dull routine of life's labor, and give out a larger measure of genial humor to gladden the lives of others, than is granted to most other men, everybody knows. And this has been with him more than a natural gift. It has been a *principle* of life. He has cultivated it. He has made it a law of his intercourse with men to be genial ; to shed a ray of sunshine upon their pathway : to put a little sweetness into their cup. He has believed that it did men good to laugh—that a pleasant smile and a cheery word are helpful to their lives : that a frowning face and harsh words can and ought to be laughed out of countenance. Who has ever heard from him the petulant retort ? Who has ever gone from his presence nursing a wound made by any word of his, spoken thoughtlessly or with deliberate intent? He has taught himself that highest achievement of self control—to maintain a perfect equanimity in the presence of every provocation, and to return the "soft answer which turneth away wrath." And he accepts

these testimonials as an evidence that this community appreciates his
endeavor to make his life a pleasure, and his presence a gleam of sunshine, upon the lives of others.

Third, he accepts them as an evidence that his life and work have
been of some service to this community; that they have contributed
something of real and permanent value to its highest interests.   He
has given twenty-five years, the prime and vigor of his manhood, to
the work of the ministry among you.   He has been abundant in
labors.   He has taken part in almost every good work that has been
carried forward in the interests of the church, and of society, in these
cities.   In his own pulpit, in other pulpits, in the homes of his people,
in the general work of the church to which he belongs, in the common
work of the churches, in the educational interests of the cities, in the
Christian charities, in the reform movements, in *every work* which has
had for its object the good of men, Dr. Reid has had some share, and
in many of them a leading and prominent part.   He has given his
counsel and lent his aid to a larger number of the moral and religious
enterprises of this community, during the past twenty-five years, than
perhaps any other living man.   And it is peculiarly pleasant to him to
read in these testimonials tendered to him to-night, the assurances that
in the judgment of that large constituency, which you, Mr. Chairman,
and gentlemen, represent, he has not labored in vain; that his service
has contributed something to the advancement of the welfare of those
whom he has tried to serve.

And in his name I thank you for these assurances.   They speak to
his heart, not only awakening grateful memories of the past, but also
inspiring him with new courage and hope for the future.   And I think
I can safely make the pledge for him to you to-night, that if the prayer
of all our hearts shall be granted, and his life shall be spared among
you for another twenty-five years of service, when the silver sheen of
this quarter centennial occasion shall have been changed into the
mellow radiance of the golden hues of his semi-centennial, he will lay
at your feet an offering of lofty purpose achieved, and service rendered,
which will claim at your hands a higher meed of praise and tribute of
acknowledgment than even that which you have so gracefully tendered
him to-night.

A few closing words were then spoken by the pastor.

CLOSING WORDS.

BY THE PASTOR.

First of all, I express my thanks to the members of the congregation for the many evidences of affection and confidence extended to me to-day. Nor have these evidences been confined to this day; they have been plentiful through all the twenty-five years of our relation. Very early in my pastorate, almost before I became accustomed to the name of pastor, the United States selected me, by lot, to the high honor of serving in the rank and file of its army. The congregation at once placed itself between me and the "draft," and purchased me and my services for the goodly price of three hundred pieces of silver. From that time till this, many valuable gifts have revealed the feelings of the people for their pastor. But these gifts, prized as they are, are not prized so highly as the kindly words which have been spoken, and the uniform confidence which has been manifested. Gathering up in memory all these evidences of affection and confidence, I say, with all the emphasis of sincere words and a full heart, I thank you.

In behalf of the congregation and myself, I thank our many friends for the words of kindness so gracefully expressed by word and by letter. It encourages us in our labors for our common Master to know that we have the esteem of those whose esteem we value. We wish for you all, pastors and people, the grace of our Lord Jesus Christ in still greater measure than we have enjoyed it.

One thing seems to have been omitted in the general congratulations of the day. Nothing has been said by way of sympathy with the congregation in the patience with which they bore, for many years, the imperfections and crudities of a "prentice hand" in preaching the Gospel. Preaching, like every other profession, must be learned in large measure by experience. It is to be hoped that the pastor has made some progress in this respect, for there was need of it; the sermons of those early days were not models. An old lady of our number, who some years ago entered into rest, and who had been trained in the Covenanter Church, and you know, Mr. Chairman, that the Covenanters were good judges of preaching, was accustomed, now and then, to take me to task if my conduct did not agree with her notions of right. On one occasion, she reproved me for permitting a young beginner to occupy the pulpit. I defended the boy and his sermon to the best of my ability, when she replied: " Well, he may improve ; perhaps it may be with him as it was with yourself ; but when I first heard you preach, I thought it was mighty poor preaching, mighty poor preaching, Mr. Reid." It must be confessed, in the calmness of mature judgment, that the opinion was correct. Looking back over those years of inexperience, I sympathize with the congregation in all that they had to bear, but I trust that in the heaps of chaff they were able to find enough grains of wheat to keep them alive. I hope there will be more wheat and less chaff in the days to come.

Such a day as this is worth waiting twenty-five years to see. Would that our former friends, who have crossed the River, could see our joy ! Perhaps they do ; who knows ? Our relation as pastor and people has been cemented in many ways. There are few homes in which I have not been called to comfort the sick and assure the dying. Memory associates sick beds and funeral services with most of our families. We have been drawn together by unnumbered hours of pleasant social intercourse. We have been knit, heart to heart, by brotherly love and the love of a common Saviour. Twenty-five years of mutual sorrow and joy and spiritual experience have made us one. Those years seem like a few days because of the greatness of my love. I can hardly realize that the children, on whose infant faces I sprinkled the water of baptism, are taking their places among the men and women of to-day. But so it is ; time has moved rapidly. The future will seem to fly more swiftly still. It can not be long now. Changes are in the near future. Others will sit in these pews ; others will stand in this sacred desk. I do not know, I do not want to know, what coming days may have in store for us ; God knows, and he is able to lead safely whatever may befall. For this I hope and pray, that when our preaching and hearing are ended, we may be among those redeemed and glorified by the grace of God.

One thing I ask for myself from you and your successors in this congregation. When I grow old, and my steps falter, and my eyes become dim, and my mind is darkened with the clouds of age, look upon me with the tender feelings with which men look upon the ruins of ancient cities, and remember, not the faltering steps and the dim eyes and the clouded mind, but what I was before "the evil days" came. When the end comes, and I lie in my coffin, calm and peaceful after life's busy day, bring your children with you, let them

peer over the coffin's edge at the dust and ashes, and as you go away
tell them: "That man, for many years, preached to us the Gospel of
the Son of God in its simplicity and purity." When I lie buried in
that plot of ground in yonder cemetery, which we are called to visit so
often, if God will vouchsafe to me this coveted privilege, surrounded
by those whom I once loved and whom I am loving yet, as you pass
by and read my name on the marble, give me a place in your thoughts
and memory side by side with my revered and saintly predecessors
Henderson, Bruce, Anderson, Lee, Reed. I ask no greater earthly
reward and honor than to be remembered by you and your children as
one of those "who have spoken unto you the word of God." Farewell.

Prayer was offered by Rev. D. S. Littell, pastor of
the Second Church, and before the benediction was pronounced, the congregation united in singing this dox-
ology, Psalm 72 : 11-12, L. M.

> Now blessed be the mighty One,
> Jehovah, God of Israel,
> For He alone hath wonders done,
> And deeds in glory that excel.
>
> And blessed be His glorious name,
> Long as the ages shall endure.
> O'er all the earth extend His fame.
> Amen, amen, forevermore.

CONGRATULATORY LETTERS.

FROM MRS M. M. BARKLEY.

ARGYLE, March 30th, 1887.

My Dear Nephew.—Not quite a year ago I received a paper from you containing your twenty-fourth anniversary sermon. After reading it, I thought, who will be here to get his twenty-fifth anniversary sermon? Yesterday I received the invitation to your quarter centennial celebration. So we are still all spared, the monuments of God's mercies, and have had through the year "a prosperous journey by the will of God." For this let us thank him. How well I would like to attend the meeting. You have a fine programme, and I shall think much about you on the afternoon and evening of April 7th. In your last year's sermon you said something like this: "The figure of the stewardship reveals especially our responsibility and accountability." And how much these anniversaries do remind us of our responsibility to God. I am often overwhelmed with the retrospect. My wasted time, my neglected opportunities, my hurtful influence, duties not performed, and as Moody said, "my laziness in God's service," and many others rise up before me, so that I am lost in wonder at God's long-suffering patience and kindness. A pastorate of a quarter of a century is rather a rare thing, but as you look backward no doubt the time seems short. You have seen many changes; but few are in the church that were there when you were installed their pastor; in your own home, too, for two of your dear ones "sleep in that low, green tent whose curtains never outward swing." May you, dear Willie, long be spared to go out and in before your people, breaking unto them the bread of life, and leading them where time is not measured by years, but to be "forever with the Lord." I thank you for this invitation, and with much love to you all, I am, as ever, affectionately,

M. M. BARKLEY.

FROM REV. W. W. BARR, D. D.

1425 CHRISTIAN ST., PHILA., April 1st, 1887.

A. M. BROWN, ESQ.—

Dear Sir:—Many thanks for your kind invitation to attend the services in commemoration of the twenty-fifth anniversary of the pastorate of my brother, the Rev. W. J. Reid, D. D. Please extend my congratulations to Dr. Reid, and the congregation, and say to them that, if it were possible, I would rejoice with them in person on the happy occasion. Denied this privilege, I must content myself with imagining the good time you will all have at your quarter centennial.

I may add that if you can get brother Reid's ear privately, you may whisper in it that I am somewhat relieved to know that there is at least one other minister in our church, beside myself, who is so unpopular that he had to stay twenty-five years with his congregation, because he could not get any other people induced to take him off their hands. Such misery courts the consolation of fellowship. Yours very truly,

W. W. BARR.

FROM REV. J. B. DALES, D. D.

136 NORTH 18th ST., PHILA., April 4th, 1887.

MR. A. M. BROWN, ESQ.—

Dear Sir:—I am very much obliged for the invitation of your Committee of Arrangements for me to be present at the celebration of the quarter centennial anniversary of the pastorate of my valued friend and brother, the Rev. Dr. Reid. But I regret to have to say that, much as I would rejoice to attend, it will not be in my power to do so.

Most cordially, however, do I send my thanksgivings to God, and my congratulations to Dr. Reid, for his long and able and useful ministry to your people, and for his various important services to the church and the cause of God at large. I congratulate your people, also, in having enjoyed so long, in these changeable times, the labor and oversight of such a servant of God—such a minister of Christ— and in many respects such a model man.

And now for both pastor and people, I give my most earnest heart's desire and prayers to God that this very marked pastoral relation may still long continue, and that of very many in that congregation and community Dr. Reid may be able in the great day to say, "these are children whom God hath given me." With every good wish, I am

Very truly yours,

J. B. DALES.

FROM REV. JAMES P. LYTLE, D. D.

SAGO, OHIO, March 28th, 1887.

A. M. BROWN, ESQ.—

Dear Sir :—Your invitation to attend the twenty-fifth anniversary of Dr. Reid's pastorate is received and welcomed.

Mrs. Lytle is at this time putting on her robes to go, before long, to the "Palace of the King," to attend an entertainment provided for her and a great many other invited guests. This will prevent myself and any of my family from attending the anniversary, to which you have kindly invited us.

Having known something of the faith which dwelt in Dr. Reid's mother Elizabeth, and in his father John, and I am persuaded that in him also, it would have given us great pleasure to have been present with you at the anniversary, had our circumstances been different.

Yours truly,

JAMES P. LYTLE.

FROM REV. S. F. MORROW, D. D.

ALBANY, N. Y., April 5th, 1887.

A. M. BROWN, Esq., Chairman of Committee of Arrangements.— .

My Dear Sir .—I much regret that I will not be able to attend the interesting services to be held on the 7th inst., in commemoration of the twenty-fifth anniversary of the pastorate of Rev. Dr. Reid. But I join in hearty congratulations to both pastor and people on the arrival of such a day. It is somewhat unusual, in this age of restlessness and change, for a minister to preach the gospel to the same people for a quarter of a century. Such an event is worthy of being celebrated in song and in festival. And my prayer is, that the relation, which has existed so long and so happily, may yet be continued for many years, and be crowned with rich blessings in the future, as it has been in the past, and like the marriage relation be dissolved only by death. And when the day of dissolution shall come, may the faithful servant be welcomed into the joy of the Lord, and be found among those who, having turned many to righteousness, "shall shine as the stars forever and ever."   Cordially yours,

S. F. MORROW.

FROM REV. SYLVESTER F. SCOVEL, PRESIDENT OF WOOSTER UNIVERSITY.

My Dear Mr. Reid :—Looking up at me from the long-read columns of the Gazette, are your well known outlines of face, and below them the expressions of your life convictions : and all serve to recall your life and speech, since I knew both, less than four years after the beginning of your pastorate.

The solid quarter of a century is a testimonial, first of all to the " Changeless Gospel," but also an emphasis upon the depth of your convictions, the fervor of your affections, and the patient strength of your work. You were a strength to us all, in the ministry and out of it, a help in every good work, charitable or educational, the friend that wisely warned or kindly approved.

I turn back the leaves of my mental diary and find your name entered upon it often, and always with the pleasantest memories attached.

You will forgive, I know, the intrusion of these lines; and may the many such bits of gratitude, which will be now reaching you, cheer your heart for all that remains in the "kingdom and patience of our Lord." Affectionately yours,

SYLVESTER F. SCOVEL.

FROM REV. D. M. URE, D. D.

MONMOUTH, ILL., April 4, 1887.

REV. W. J. REID, D. D. :—

My Dear Brother :—It would give me great pleasure to attend the anniversary of your twenty-five years' pastorate. But I cannot ; I have been, and am, exceedingly busy. Nor will I be in time to send my regrets to the committee in charge. But I want to write you personally a few words of congratulation.

The situation was not full of promise when you accepted the call of the First Church, Pittsburgh. It was a remnant merely, the ruins, I might say, of a once prosperous church. There was no prestige about it at that time, but rather something, perhaps, of a stigma as a quarrelsome people. In the membership, there remained little of the warm blood and enthusiasm of youth ; much more of the decrepitude of age. It was a "down-town church," in the midst of business blocks, and convenient to hotel and depot ; but far from the homes which have the material for congregational growth, and with which the pastor has most to do. But through all these years, the members of the First Church have been harmonious, and pastor and people have been "striving together," and not against one another, " for the furtherance of the Gospel." Long ago the remnant had grown into a large and flourishing congregation, though most of the people have had so far to go to make it their church home.

Though the situation has been so unfavorable, and a multitude have gone to many other localities in search of better worldly condition, not a few to glory, its members are, I believe, maintained from year to year. Those who have had much to do with congregations will best recognize the uncommon wisdom, prudence, care and patience necessary on the part of the pastor to these twenty-five years of harmony and brotherly co-operation. Then what large demands have been made upon talent, upon educational resources, upon reading and study by the pulpit, by the prayer meetings, by the Sabbath school, by the house of mourning, not to speak of the responsibilities of a minister in such a city, beyond the congregation proper! At the close of a quarter century of successful service, in all departments, you are, my brother, a phenomenon in the pastorate !

The difficulties of the position, and the restlessness of the times, make pastorates usually brief; and they are becoming more so. He who wins success, where so many fail, in maintaining an important pastorate, and all the time adding to its influence, is a hero in his sphere. And where is there a nobler sphere, or a hero more deserving appreciation and honor ?

Joining with your hosts of friends in congratulations, in gratitude to our God for the help that has enabled you to be useful, and in best wishes and prayers for your future, I remain

Yours in Christian Bonds,
D. M. URE.

FROM REV. ALEX. G. WALLACE, D. D., CORRESPONDING SECRETARY OF THE BOARD OF CHURCH EXTENSION.

SEWICKLEY, PA:, April 7, 1887.

REV. WILLIAM J. REID, D. D.:—

My Very Dear Brother :—Permit me to join with your congregation in the rejoicings of to-day.

Parallel to the line of the twenty-five years of your pastoral relation and work, and for nearly the whole length of it, has been the line of a

personal friendship which does not show a single break or even a blur
—a friendship which has been to me precious and valuable, unreserved
and tender. I am deeply thankful to God, that in the closeness of
relation created by our common work, in the intimacy of confidential
friendship, there is not anything in the past, on your part, to give a
moment's pain, and that with all my faults and shortcomings you are
still the kind, trusting brother you have always been. Your house has
been a home to me; your family are dear to me; your sorrow is our
sorrow. I rejoice in all that God has done by you, and in all that
makes your heart glad.

The Lord bless and keep you and yours. May no sorrow come to
you, but ever growing joy and peace, is the prayer of all my family.

Your Brother,

A. G. WALLACE.

FROM REV. CHARLES A. DICKEY, D. D.

1814 PINE ST., PHILA., April 5, 1887.

My Dear Billy,—Is there not some mistake about this "quarter
centennial" business? Can it be that twenty-five years separate us
from those memorable evenings that seemed so full of interest to you
and me? On Monday night, I sat silent and thoughtful, and rejoiced
in the expectation of working side by side with one who had become
my close friend, in the intimacy of seminary life. Tuesday night you
came over, and, if I remember right, you laid hands upon me, in the
ordination. It seems but yesterday, and yet you have announced that
twenty-five years of work and care, of love and change, have come
and gone since then. Providences have separated our works, but no
changes have separated our lives and hearts. The years have been
filled with many toils, but they have been overflowing cups of mercies.
I congratulate you that you "abide in the love of your people." Your
faithful work is your crown of honor. I pray that these *silver* lines
may turn to *gold*, and that we may have our semi-centennial in the
kingdom of Christ, here or at home. Affectionately yours,

CHARLIE.

FROM REV. JOHN S. SANDS, D. D.

1014 RACE ST., PHILA., April 6, 1887.

My Dear Dr. Reid:—Absence from the city prevented me from
acknowledging before now the receipt of an invitation to the quarter

centennial anniversary of your installation. I love you, and regret that I am so far away that I can not sit under your big shadow for a little while on Thursday. For thirteen years out of the twenty-five, you and I laughed and cried together, and few weeks passed in which we did not see each other. You know what a long letter I could write, if I undertook to put on paper my thoughts about the quarter century of service, or the thirteen years of brotherly fellowship. But your mail will be very heavy these days, and I must not do more than send to you, on this happy anniversary, and to your good people, into whose faces I would like to look, and to the faithful wife at your side, my earnest and prayerful congratulations. You will be honored to-day, deservedly so, and most heartily do I rejoice with you. But better still, when the Chief Shepherd shall appear, you will receive a crown of glory that fadeth not away. So will I; and then we will humbly rejoice together, as we talk over the "days of old, the years departed long."

> "O honor higher, truer far
> Than earthly fame could bring,
> Thus to be used in work like this,
> So long, by such a King!"

"The Lord bless you and keep you. The Lord make his face to shine upon you and be gracious unto you. The Lord lift up his countenance upon you and give you peace." Sincerely yours in the bonds of brotherhood,

JOHN S. SANDS.

FROM REV. A. W. MORRIS.

SOUTH ARGYLE, N. Y., April 5, 1887.

THE COMMITTEE OF ARRANGEMENTS, ETC.:—

Gentlemen:—Nothing could afford us greater pleasure than to be present at the services to be held in commemoration of the twenty-fifth anniversary of Dr. Reid's pastorate in the First Church, Pittsburgh. But circumstances forbid. We congratulate you all on this anniversary, and express the hope that the second quarter century may witness a growing affection between the parties concerned, if not any marked growth in the visible proportions. May both pastor and people be spared, and so guided by a kind Providence, that they may pass together the seventh of April for many years to come, is the prayer of   Yours truly,

A. W. MORRIS.

FROM PROFESSOR J. F. McCLYMONDS.

ATWOOD, PA., April 5. 1887.

TO THE COMMITTEE OF ARRANGEMENTS :—

I hereby acknowledge the receipt of your invitation to attend the services in commemoration of the twenty-fifth anniversary of the pastorate of Dr. Reid. It would afford me much pleasure to comply with your invitation ; but it may not be; circumstances beyond my control prevent it. Though absent in body, I shall be present in spirit. I admire the feeling on the part of the congregation that prompted it to tender to its pastor its gratitude in such a delicate and appropriate manner.

Humanly speaking, he is worthy of all the gratitude your hearts are capable of expressing. Hold up his hands in every possible way ; encourage his heart by every act of kindness your generosity can suggest.

May the First Church, Pittsburgh, and its pastor, journey on together until the fiftieth milestone in their journey is reached, and during all this time may " brotherly love continue." When Dr. Reid stands before the great white throne on the day of final assizes, may his heart be a thousand times gladder than it possibly can be on the 7th of April, 1887. May he and all that have enjoyed his ministry hear in that day the welcome, " Well done, good and faithful servants, enter into the joy of thy Lord." Yours most sincerely.

J. F. McCLYMONDS.

FROM REV. A. CALHOUN, D. D.

SAN JOSE, CAL., April 2, 1887.

Dear Brother Reid :—I have just received, by the " Committee of Arrangements," an invitation to attend the services contemplated in connection with the twenty-fifth anniversary of your pastorate.

On account of distance I cannot be present, but send you the assurance of my hearty congratulations. The fact, that this celebration takes place, is proof that as to pastor and people there has been mutual worth, love and fidelity. That this relationship, with Divine approbation, may continue for many years to come, is the prayer of your former fellow presbyter,

A. CALHOUN.

P. S.—On these occasions the pastor generally receives more than his share of pleasant remembrances. On this occasion, I wish to be understood as tendering to the pastor's wife congratulations as cordial as those tendered her worthy husband.

A. C.

FROM A FORMER MEMBER.

April 7, 1887.

DR. WILLIAM J. REID:—

My Dear Friend :—I wish to add this small check to the amount contributed by your congregation. There was a woman, once in the membership of your church, and now, we trust, in the membership of the church above, who was your friend. She looks on to-night with approval, and I want my dear mother to be remembered in the pleasure of this occasion. Very truly your friend.

* * * *

FROM REV. JAMES Y. BOICE.

2213 SPRING GARDEN, PHILA., April 11, 1887.

REV. W. J. REID, D. D.:—

My Dear Brother :—In this morning's mail, there came to me the programme of the quarter centennial anniversary of your installation as pastor of the First Church. I hope you will not look upon me as an intruder if I venture to do what my heart prompts me to do—send you my very sincere congratulations in view of this most interesting occasion. You will kindly allow me to say that the man who can stand in one pulpit for twenty-five years is no ordinary man. I remember quite well your coming to the First Church, and the early years of your ministry there. And I have many and precious reasons for doing so.

You are one among a few who have had a marked influence upon my life. The touch of one man upon the life of another is vastly different from the touch of another upon that same life.

Especially do I recall with great pleasure the Bible class you were accustomed to teach on Sabbath afternoons in the lecture room of your church. The subject of study on those occasions was the gospel of Christ by John. This moment I picture to myself the scene ; the pews filled with young people having open Bibles in their hands, your rapid and cheerful movement from seat to seat with questions designed to bring out the meaning of the Word, your tender thoughtfulness with those who manifested some hesitancy in answering, your brief announcement about the meeting on the next Sabbath afternoon and cordial invitation to come. Those hours were full of interest and instruction to me. Nor am I unmindful of the many and precious afternoons which your kindness of heart prompted you to give me for my instruction in Greek. I am sure your patience was tried by your dull pupil. But I am thankful for those afternoons. I am sure that I am a better man because of them. The memory of them is sweet to me. They brought me much more than the simple knowledge of the Greek text.

The exercises on Thursday must have been delightful. I was most happy to note the hearty and substantial manner in which your people and the community indicated their appreciation of you. Major A. M. Brown's address was admirable, and your own closing words were unutterably affecting. I wanted to tell you in this note the profit I have derived from your published works. They have been and are to me a source of most valuable instruction. Your lectures on the Revelation are indeed good reading : and your book—United Presbyterianism—I value highly as an exposition of the faith of the church. With kind regards to yourself and Mrs. Reid and family, I am your brother in the Gospel.

JAMES Y. BOICE.

TWENTY-FIFTH ANNIVERSARY SERMON.

PREACHED APRIL 3, 1887, BY THE PASTOR, WILLIAM J. REID, D. D.

" But though we, or an angel from heaven, preach any other gospel unto you than that which we have preached unto you, let him be accursed."—Gal. 1 : 8.

Twenty-five years! A quarter of a century! The words are short, but the time they describe is long. The syllables are soon spoken, but they measure a large portion of an earthly life. It is with peculiar feelings I stand in my place to-day and preach my twenty-fifth anniversary sermon. Memory is busy; love is quickened ; regrets are multiplied ; hope is revived. Absent but unforgotten faces are seen ; silent voices are heard ; the heart throbs with affection for those whom we once loved and whom we are loving yet; neglected opportunities rise, like ghosts, to affright the soul. With all, thoughts of a better future comfort and cheer. The day is a day of mingled emotions. The mountain, on which we stand, is one on which the noise of many thunders blends with the still, small voice of hope. Perhaps the one thought, which most strongly takes possession of our minds at such a time as this, has to do with the changes which fill our years. Our world is

A WORLD OF CHANGES,

and anniversary days bring these changes into prominence. There are changes in the natural world. Cloud and sunshine give endless variety ; day and night chase each other with tireless feet around the circle of the heavens. We hardly become familiar with the driving snows and ice-bound streams of the winter, before hill and valley are covered with the verdure of summer; and then the summer's verdure, as with the wave of a magician's wand, gives place to the desolation of December. There are changes in the political world. New rulers take the places of those who are called away ; the boundaries of king- doms are so altered, that we can scarcely recognize the continents of our school days on the maps which our children are studying. There are changes in our homes. We fail to see the children of yesterday in the busy men and graceful women of to-day. There are changes in the life of the individual. " The times have changed and we have changed in them." There are changes in the congregational life, with which we are brought face to face on every anniversary. The twenty-five years we remember to-day have wrought wonders. Of the Session at the beginning of my pastorate, only two are tarrying, and only one of these is now a member of Session. Of the 119 persons who signed my call, only 51 are alive, and only 29 are connected with the congregation. Of the 170 persons who were then reported as members, 16 were wrongly reported; of the 154 others, only 36 are now enrolled among our living members. Those who were then old have one by one departed; those who were then in the prime of life are now wearing the crown of gray hairs; those who were then children are taking their place in the front rank of life's activities.

This world of ours is a world of changes. Is there anything unchanging? We long for something which will abide. We cannot find it in ourselves; we cannot find it in our surroundings. We are like the dove which Noah sent out from his ark—the fickle and changing waves are beneath us and around us; we must find somewhere a stable peak of granite, or we can never rest. Where shall we look? In what direction shall we turn? If we wish for something abiding, something on which we can rest with unshaken confidence through all the vicissitudes of life, we must find it in God, who never changes, or in the gospel of his Son, which, like its divine Author, is "the same yesterday, to-day and forever."

THE UNCHANGING GOSPEL

is the theme which I have chosen for my anniversary sermon, and which I would impress upon your memory and conscience with all the emphasis of twenty-five years of experience. Paul knew that the gospel he had preached to the Galatians would remain the only true gospel till the end of time. Therefore he said, "Though we or an angel from heaven preach any other gospel unto you than that which we have preached unto you, let him be accursed." What was this gospel which he so confidently announced as the unchanging and unchangeable gospel? We may learn what it was from a study of Paul's life, and from a study of the life and work of Jesus, whose Apostle Paul was. May I not take it for granted that you know what are the fundamental doctrines of this gospel? Will it not be sufficient for me, now and here, to read only the head-lines of our confession of faith? First, every man is a sinner, and sin deserves the wrath and curse of God; second, God so loved the world that he gave his only begotten Son; third, the Son of God suffered and died, the just for the unjust; fourth, men are justified by faith in the crucified but now risen Son of God. Or, if you wish a briefer statement, it is this:—Salvation is through faith in Christ.

This is the unchanging gospel, a gospel of human sin, of divine love, of a suffering Substitute and of justifying faith. The men to whom it is preached may change, and must change, but the same gospel is preached to their children and their children's children. The preachers who preach it may change, and must change; the voice of one is heard for a little while and then it dies away in silence, but a new voice cries the same message. One man may put more emphasis on one word than another, but it is the same gospel. The message may be spoken in different languages, but it voices the same truth. Go back through the ages of history; over all the crash and roar of earth's many battle fields, over the wild shrieks which pain wrings from human lips, over the discordant voices of trade and the sturdy blows of labor, over the boisterous laugh of innocent gayety and the profane song of riotous living, there is heard, loud and clear as an angel's trumpet, this word of the gospel, "Neither is there salvation in any other." Jerusalem heard these words before its temple and its palaces went down in fire and blood; the banks of Jordan and the shores of Galilee listened and were glad; Paul preached them in learned Athens, in impure Corinth and in pagan Rome; they echoed through the darkness of the middle ages; they were heard in the mountains and glens of Scotland; they were graven on Plymouth Rock; they are spoken to-day by thousands of tongues in every land. Paul and Peter, Luther and Calvin, Knox and Wesley, Edwards and Mason, all the rest of the uncounted host of the faithful dead, and all their disciples who are now in the land of the living, may differ widely in other things, but they are alike in that this is the burden of their message to the sinful world, "Neither is there salvation in any other."

The argument in favor of the divine origin of our holy religion, founded on the well known fact that the gospel has remained unchanged through all the ages, has not perhaps received the attention which its importance deserves. Other systems of belief and practice have been modified by human need, by increasing knowledge, and by force of circumstances. Astronomy is a different science now from what it was when Paul preached on Mars' Hill. Geology has changed its teachings more than once within the memory of men now living. One school of mental philosophy has followed another, each one demolishing the principles which its predecessor had builded. Political science has had to adapt itself to the peculiarities of different people. But the gospel is the same always and everywhere: at Abraham's altar, in Moses' tabernacle, in Solomon's temple, in Jewish synagogue, and in Christian church; in "Greenland's icy mountains," and on "India's coral strand;" in the crowded city and the lonely forest; in the palace of the king and the cottage of the peasant; in the university of learning and the workshop. There is not one gospel for the Jew and another for the Gentile, one for the rich and another for the poor, one for Europe and another for America. Its unvarying words are, "He that believeth shall be saved." That gospel which never needs to change, and which is adapted to men of every clime and class, must be divine: it must be the work of Him "with whom is no variableness, neither shadow of turning." And as the gospel has never changed, we may conclude that it will never change. Paul was confident that what he preached would be preached to the end of the world. We may have the same confidence. Kingdoms may rise and fall; generations may come and go; art and science may make greater advancement than they have made since the beginning; but the message of the gospel will ever be, "Neither is there salvation in any other."

ANOTHER GOSPEL.

Every reader of history must know that this is not the only gospel which has been preached and believed. Paul tells us that there is another gospel, "which is not another." There is but one gospel, and any other system of faith which claims for itself this name is stealing the livery of heaven to serve the devil in. God has given the name "gospel" to the plan of salvation through Christ, and no offspring of the human brain has the right to appropriate this name. However, we may, for the sake of convenience, imitate Paul's example and call every rival of the true gospel "another gospel."

The other gospel, which bewitched the "foolish Galatians," and moved the Apostle's indignation, was that men must be circumcised and keep the law of Moses, or they would not be saved. This gospel did not long survive. In a few years after this epistle was written, there was not a professing Christian anywhere on earth, who thought that obedience to the ceremonial law was necessary to salvation. But though this particular form of error was short-lived, others took its place. Some have preached the necessity of good works as a ground of justification; some have preached that Jesus is not a sufficient intercessor, and that there is need of the intercession of saints and angels; some have preached that the sacrifice of Christ on the cross was not complete, and that it must be supplemented by penance and the daily

sacrifice of the mass; some have preached that Jesus of Nazareth was
not the Son of God, but only a good man and a successful teacher;
some have preached that this life does not decide the destiny of men,
and that there is a second probation. But any attempt to mention,
one by one, the other gospels which have been preached on earth, and
which have followed each other in rapid succession, must be in vain.
It must suffice to say that any so-called gospel, which does not hold up
Christ as the sufficient and only Saviour, is one of those other gospels
of which Paul speaks when he says:—"Though we, or an angel from
heaven preach any other gospel unto you than that which we have
preached unto you, let him be accursed."

NO NEED FOR ANOTHER GOSPEL.

Which gospel has been preached to you during the past twenty-five
years? The unchanging gospel, or another gospel? I am willing to
leave the answering of this question to your consciences. I have
nothing to say as to the manner in which the gospel has been preached;
no one can have a more vivid appreciation of its imperfections than
the preacher himself; but I am sure of this, the gospel has been
preached in its purity; Jesus has been held up as the only Saviour of
sinners. I claim no praise for myself but for the gospel preached when
I say, if those who have listened to the sermons delivered in this pulpit
would obey the things which they have heard, not one would be lost;
all without exception would enter glory at last. Though " our gospel "
has not been fully obeyed, our history during the past quarter of a
century adds its testimony to the testimony of all the preceding cen-
turies that there is no need of another gospel. The unchanging gospel,
which Paul preached in Galatia, has shown itself adapted to our circumstances and sufficient for our needs. We may test its power and
efficacy by the experience of twenty-five years. A quarter of a century
may seem a short time; it is a short time when compared with the
unending future; nevertheless, sixteen consecutive pastorates of equal
length would carry us back to the birth of Luther, and seventy-five
would bring us to the day of the Saviour's crucifixion.

A REVIEW OF TWENTY-FIVE YEARS

will prove the sufficiency of the gospel to convert souls, edify saints
and build up the church. At the beginning of my pastorate 170
persons were reported as belonging to the congregation, though 16 of
them had previously withdrawn. Since that time 293 have been received on the profession of their faith and 546 on certificate, making a
total of 839, During the same time 581 names have been removed

from the roll by death, dismission and otherwise, leaving our present membership 428. What led all these persons to make a profession of their faith and keep up their connection with the church? It was the unchanging gospel, brought to bear on their hearts and consciences by the preaching of the pulpit, the teaching of the Sabbath school and the instruction of the home. In so far as they were true Christians, and in the judgment of Christian charity we will hope that they were what they professed to be, they were converted by the Spirit using different human instrumentalities, but always the same gospel. Some of them were young, others were old; some were learned, others unlearned; some had been trained in Christian homes, others were brought in from the world. In this respect the gospel has been no respecter of persons; it has proved itself adapted to the wants of every one who would accept it.

The gospel has also been instrumental in edifying saints. The matter of edification can not be expressed in figures and statistics. We can not measure sanctification by the line and plummet. But that saints have been edified during these years may not be denied. There have been instances of growth in grace too manifest to be doubted. I have seen men and women growing in knowledge, faith, patience, obedience and all the graces of the Spirit, until they could bear their trials and perform their duties and glorify their God in the very spirit of the Divine Master. Would to God that their number was increased! No matter how much we must lament our short-comings, we must know that there has been growth in grace, and that this growth has been caused by the unchanging gospel.

Of course, there is reason for humiliation here. If pastor and people had been more faithful, more sinners would have been converted; if we had been more diligent in using the means appointed for our edification, we would have made higher attainments in the divine life. But what has been done proves that the gospel has lost none of its power. Whatever lack there may be is not in it, but in ourselves. The experience of the past twenty-five years demonstrates that we need no other gospel for the conversion of sinners and the edification of saints. If I had the quarter of a century to live over again, I would preach nothing but Christ and him crucified as the only sufficient Saviour.

Twenty-five years of experience have also shown the sufficiency of the gospel to attract and hold the attention of men. During my pastorate I have preached 1,774 sermons at home and 914 in other places, making a total of 2,688. During the same period 625 sermons have been preached in this church by my brethren in the ministry, so that as a congregation you have listened to 2,399 sermons in the course of the present pastorate. In addition to these formal sermons, I have lectured on Wednesday evenings almost without interruption, spoken words of comfort, founded on the gospel, on those sad occasions when the dead were carried out to their burial, taught Bible classes, and told of Jesus and his love at other times and in other ways. And yet men come to hear the story of the cross. They are attracted by the gospel as nothing else could attract them. Could it be possible to draw together, in summer's heat and winter's cold, the same congregation a hundred times a year for twenty-five years, to listen to lectures on science, on literature or politics? It is true, if a distinguished states-man or a learned scientist makes an address or several addresses, multi-tudes will crowd to hear him; but if he attempts two or three addresses every week in the same place, from one year's end to another, he will soon find a diminishing audience. It is otherwise with the gospel. It is always new and attractive. Surely that gospel, which has such power to arrest and hold the attention of men, must be from God, and we need no other.

Twenty-five years of experience have also shown the sufficiency of the gospel to call out the liberality of men. It is not easy to persuade men to give away the possessions which they have earned by their skill and labor. That system of doctrine which can awaken such a spirit of liberality as will make cheerful givers must be anointed with power from on high. How has it been with us during the continuance of the present pastorate? We have raised for the Boards of the church $38,590, and for other purposes $144,951, a total of $183,541. We have been growing in this grace. During the first year we raised $248 for the Boards, and $2,537 for other purposes; during the last year $2,375 for the Boards, and $6,423 for other purposes. We have not yet reached the standard of Christian liberality, but what we have done shows that the gospel of the Son of God has lost none of its power.

Twenty-five years of experience have also shown the sufficiency of the gospel to give comfort and support in the hour of death. This is the hour which tries the soul. Many a thing, which gives great enjoy-ment in health, is worse than useless in the presence of death. Again and again has the gospel been tested in our homes during the past quarter of a century, and it has never failed to abide the test. One hundred and sixty-one of our members have entered into rest, from William McGill, who died May 8, 1862, to Elias Radcliff, who died December 24, 1886. Some of them were old and weary with the burdens of life; some of them were in the vigor of their prime; some of them were young; but not one of them found his trust in the Saviour of the gospel to be in vain. All this proves that we need no other gospel to die by, than that which has been preached unto you and which you believe.

To gather up in a brief statement the labors and results of the pastorate, it would be this:—293 have been received into the church on the profession of their faith, and 546 on certificate, a total of 839. During the same time, there has been a decrease of 581. I have preached 1,774 sermons at home, and 914 elsewhere, a total of 2,688. I have attended 639 funerals, officiated at 417 marriages, and baptized 397 children. As a congregation, we have raised $38,590 for the Boards of the church, and $144,951 for other purposes, a total of $183-251. While humbly confessing that we have left undone many things we should have done, and making grateful acknowledgment of the patience of God with us in all our short-comings in duty, we have no reason to be ashamed of the gospel of Christ, of what it has done for us and of what it has enabled us to do. In view of past experience, we may affirm with all confidence that no other gospel is needed.

THE PAST YEAR.

Our history during the past year has not been an eventful one to us as a congregation, whatever it may have been to individual members. On April 1, 1886, we reported a membership of 427. During the year there have been 19 additions, 9 by profession and 10 by certificate. During the same time 7 of our members have died and 11 other names have been removed from the roll by certificate or otherwise. This makes our membership on April 1, 1887, 428. The names of our brethren who have entered into rest during the year are:—James A. Askins, May 11; Samuel E. Herron, June 12; Mrs. Fannie Chambers, July 20; William M. Gormley, August 22; Miss Martha Wallace, September 6; Mrs. Susan Nicholson, December 23; Elias Radcliff, December 24. "Blessed are the dead which die in the Lord from henceforth: yea, saith the Spirit, that they may rest from their labors; and their works do follow them."

The money raised in the congregation during the year is as follows: From pew rent, $3,986.12; from the annual collection for the Boards, $2,051.82; from Sabbath morning collections, $685.84; on hospital Sabbath, $101.56; by special collection for Oakland, $234.07; by the Women's Missionary Society, $773.24; by the Young Women's Missionary Society, $186.20; for the Orphans' Home, $73; for the Mt. Washington Church, $135; by the Sabbath School, $280.46; for the Sabbath School, $244.38; for the Bible Society, $68; from miscellaneous sources, $46; total, $8,865.69.

The work at Oakland Chapel has outgrown our expectations. The success which has attended that effort, which is still under the immediate supervision of Rev. H. C. Marshall, seems to indicate that it was a wise movement, and that it is enjoying the blessing of God. On April 1, 1886, there were 16 members. During the year there have been 38 additions, 18 by profession and 20 by certificate. There has also been a decrease of 2, leaving the present membership 52. The Sabbath school has 22 officers and teachers, and 170 scholars; it has contributed $215. The money raised there has been as follows:—By subscriptions and collections, $1,133.25; for the Boards, $132; total, $1,265.25. We still ask for this enterprise a place in your attention, your liberality and your prayers.

And now, still preaching and hearing the same unchanging gospel, we enter upon the first year of the second quarter of a century of our relation as pastor and people. How long I will preach, and how long you will hear, is known only to God. Of the 119 persons who signed my call, the following are yet in the membership of the congregation : Samuel George, Mrs. Ann George, Mrs. Mary J. Morris, James R. Murdoch, Miss Susan Haslett, Miss Margaret Haslett, Mrs. Mary Mitchell, John McCune, Mrs. Maria McCune, Mrs. Susan Herron, Miss Mary Lowry, Miss Sarah Irvine, Mrs. Lydia Love, William Stevenson, John Park, James Park, Alexander Boyce, John B. Herron, Mrs. Annie R. Herron, James E. Dickson, Mrs. R. S. Lambert, Mrs. Lydia Rodgers, James McQuiston, Miss Ann McQuiston, Mrs. H. Littell, Mrs. Frances Neiper, Mrs. Anna Martin, Mrs. Eleanor W. Bruce, Mrs. Eliza W. Banks, Miss Emma J. Whitten. The following, though yet alive, are in connection with other congregations: John Herron, Miss Ellen Murdoch, Miss Margaret Johns, Mrs. Elizabeth Walker, Miss Mary Watson, Miss Mary J. George, Miss Mary J. Bingham, Mrs. Sarah L. White, Thomas Gibson, Henry Breene, Mrs. Mary Breene, Mrs. Sarah A. Park, John Scott, William J. McMaster, Mrs. Mary Leech, Miss Maria J. Forbes, Miss Jane McBride, William Hamilton, William Patterson, Mrs. Jane Patterson, Ebenezer McKnight, Elgin Bruce, Mrs. Mary J. Bruce, Miss Maggie Howard, Miss Elizabeth Patterson, Samuel Martin, T. J. Shaw, Mrs. E. Shaw, William Wandless, George Wandless, Jr. These are dead : John Lowry, John Graham, George Rodgers, Thomas Dickson, Thomas Mitchell, Joseph Coltart, Mrs. Jean R. Coltart, Mrs. Rachel Leech, Mrs. Margaret Miller, John Murdoch, Jr., Miss Martha Wallace, Mrs. Mary Haslett, Mrs. Elizabeth Anderson, Mrs. Mary George, Peter Duff, Mrs. Eliza Duff, Mrs. Jane Donaldson, Mrs. Susan Nicholson, Mrs. Eliza Rodg-

ers, Mrs. Mary Bingham, Miss Sarah Stewart, Miss Sarah J. Cunning-
ham, James Orr, Mrs. Maria Orr, Joseph Love, Mrs. Margaret Gibson,
John Moore, Mrs. Mary Ferguson, Mrs. Eliza Park, George B. Millar,
Mrs. Margaret Millar, William Clendining, Miss Martha Clendining,
Hugh McMaster, Mrs. Mary McMaster, Charles B. Leech, David
Johnston, Mrs. Eliza Linton, Mrs. Mary J. Dickson, Miss Susan Dick-
son, Mrs. Ruth Harper, Mrs. Agnes Coleman, Miss Sarah Coleman,
John Rodgers, R. Hamilton, Mrs. Mary McKnight, William Cham-
bers, Mrs. Frances Chambers, Alexander Dickson, Mrs. Jane G. Dick-
son, Francis Stevenson, Mrs. Jane Stevenson, Thomas Barkley,
Thomas Smith, Miss Mary Whitten, George Wandless, Sr., Mrs.
Esther Wandless, William McGill, Mrs. Jane McGill.

The dead of the past tell us that "the time is short." If we have
any undone work to do, any unattained attainments to reach, any un-
conquered spiritual foes to subdue, any preparation for the inevitable
hereafter to make, we must be up and doing, for the night is coming
when work is impossible.

It is useless to wait for a new gospel, for the gospel changes not. I
know not what weakness of mind or what temptations of Satan may be
mine in coming years. I may, if I do not firmly hold to the Master's
hand, run into the wild delusions which have misled many who have
stood in the sacred desk, and to whose intellectual powers I must bow
with profound reverence; I may preach as others have done, if the
Lord does not keep me, the foolishness of men instead of the wisdom
of God; but if I do, I ask for your pity and not for your obedience.
When I turn away from the gospel of the Son of God, turn away from
me; stop your ears and harden your hearts against any words I may
speak in that hour which, I pray, may never come. I know not who
may stand in this pulpit after my removal or decease; I hope this congregation will enjoy the labors of many pastors, more learned and
eloquent and saintly than any of their predecessors, who will lift higher
the banner of the cross than it has yet been lifted; but if any of them
should preach any other gospel unto you than that which you have
heard for twenty-five years past, though he may preach it with profound
learning and moving eloquence, listen not to his words, for they will
be poison and death. Standing to-day on the sure word of prophecy,
and looking down through the ages to the second coming of the Son
of Man, I say with the unshaken confidence of the great Apostle of the
Gentiles, "Though we, or an angel from heaven, preach any other
gospel unto you than that which we have preached unto you, let him
be accursed."

Quarter Centennial Committees.

General Committee.

Of the Session.

J. G. Templeton,   S. L. McHenry.

Of the Trustees.

A, M. Brown,   Frank G. Bryce,
James Loughridge,   R. J. McKnight,
Thomas R. Herd,   E. B. Mahood,
Samuel McMahon.

Of the Women's Missionary Societies.

Mrs. John B. Herron,   Mrs. D. D. Bruce,
Mrs. Robert Stevenson,   Miss Esther A. Stevenson,
Miss Mary Orr Lowry,   Miss Amanda Smith,
Miss Lizzie W. Porter.

Committee of Arrangements.

A. M. Brown,   Mrs. John B. Herron,
S. L. McHenry,   Miss Mary Orr Lowry,
R. J. McKnight.

RECEPTION COMMITTEE.

J. G. Templeton,
Samuel McMahon,
John B. Herron,
Frank G. Bryce,
Robert McBride,
G. Lambert Rodgers,
F. A. Stevenson,
James McQuiston,
Thomas R. Herd,
William Stevenson,
W. W. Armstrong,
A. H. Bryce,
Joseph Faloon,
James Loughridge,
Joseph S. Vincent,
W. A. Edeburn,
T. A. Elliott,
A. P. Thompson,
William McKown,

Mrs. Mary Mitchell,
Mrs. Samuel George,
Mrs. Rebecca S. Lambert,
Mrs. D. D. Bruce,
Mrs. James McMaster,
Mrs. James Bryce,
Mrs. Mary J. Morris,
Mrs. Martha Stewart,
Mrs. Hanna Littell,
Miss Mary Lowry,
Miss Sarah Irvine,
Miss Ann McQuiston,
Miss Agnes D. Ferguson,
Miss Agnes Wandless,
Miss Mary D. Young,
Miss Amanda Smith,
Miss Margaret Haslett,
Miss Jennie E. Thompson,
Miss Martha H. McMaster.

INDEX.